BUNK!

Written by Pete Barnstrom & Jamie Nash

Illustrations by Jeff Cerica & Lauren Hanchin

SKYPATH

BUNK by Pete Barnstrom & Jamie Nash
Published by Skypath Media
277 Royal Poinciana Way, #152
Palm Beach, FL 33480
http://www.skypathmedia.com/

Illustrations by Jeff Cerica & Lauren Hanchin

Cover Illustration by Gracie Taylor. Follow her on facebook @ graydoodles17 or visit her website at gracie-taylor.squarespace.com

Book interior & cover design by Susan Mangan
smangan@what-design.com

978-0-9990913-0-2 (paperback)
978-0-9990913-1-9 (ebook)

BUNK!

Contents

CHAPTER ONE
HOME

When Mom and Dad picked me up from the Girl Scout camp bus, they said there was a big surprise waiting for me at home. But I couldn't have expected the Bunkmobile.

No one expects the Bunkmobile!

"What?" I said.

"Is?" I said.

"THAT?" I said. And I might have been a little louder than I needed to be.

That's my Uncle Danny. If there were a family vote, he would win the "Most Likely To Be Driving Something Like This Monstrosity" award.

"I call it the Bunkmobile!" he shouted proudly, like a circus ringmaster.

"The Bunkmobile? Because our name is Bunkhouse?" I asked.

"Huh. Didn't think about that. That's good." Uncle Danny shrugged. "But I called it the Bunkmobile because it has beds. Get it — bed, bunks, bunk, bed. The Bedmobile wasn't as catchy."

"Hold up. There's beds in that thing?" I tried to peer through the grime-caked windows.

"There's beds all right. In fact, there's one for you." Dad rested a hand on my shoulder. "You're going to be spending the rest of the summer in the Bunkmobile, driving across the country with Uncle Danny."

I gasped.

Don't get me wrong. I love Uncle Danny. He's super cool.

But I had plans. Girl plans.

My BFF Chloe and I had loaded up our schedule with girls-only fun, including (but not limited to) karaoke, watching movies, painting nails, dance parties, mall hangs, sleepovers, and horseback riding. Just the two of us. No boys, no Girl Scout drama, minimal parents, and lots and lots of bedazzling. It was to be our one last summer before we went off to become middle school women.

But Mom and Dad had plans of their own. And an itinerary. In fact, they had tickets. Two tickets. Destination: Hawaii. Which, if you are as math-challenged as I am, means just them, and not me.

So much for bedazzling.

Still, when Uncle Danny announced that the first stop on our road trip was going to be Pirate Pete's Pillaging Play-Park and Petting Zoo, I perked up.

Me likey the rollercoasters. (And alliteration.)

Later that afternoon, as Uncle Danny glided the Bunkmobile into the Pirate Pete's parking lot, I could already smell the cotton candy and barf.

"Let's go," I shouted and climbed out of the RV. "The sooner I get in line, the sooner I start screaming upside down!"

"Yeah, hold up, Berni," Uncle Danny took my hand. "We're not here to ride the Brain Scrambler."

"That's okay, I'll settle for the Tilt-A-Hurl. I hear it slings you around so fast, you're actually an inch taller after you get off!"

"Berni, I have to tell you something." Uncle Danny knelt down to my eye level.

"I know, I know," I put my hand on my heart as if I was saying the Pledge of Allegiance. "I, Berni Bunkhouse, being of sound mind and body, do hereby promise not to get lost, run away, or T-bone old grannies with bumper cars. I also solemnly swear to keep my arms and legs inside the vehicle at all times."

4

"No," he shook his head. "Not that. I mean, sure, that. But there's something I didn't tell you about this little road trip."

A roar of laughter caught my attention. Well, not quite a roar, but more than a collection of giggles. Call it a roar-let.

A crowd was on their feet clapping and whistling, standing around a ramshackle stage set up in the area beside the entry gates.

A boy stood alone on the stage.

"Wait, I know that magician..." I said.

"... is that... Baxter the Magnificent?"

"That's what I wanted to talk to you about," Uncle Danny said.

My heart pounded. That face. That *horrible* face. I'd seen it in every nightmare since my eighth birthday party. The party we don't talk about. The one of which I demanded all my guests delete every picture and video from their phones and cameras.

My hands balled into fists. "Why is Baxter the Magnificent here on my summer vacation? What have I done to deserve this?"

"His parents have summer plans, so I told them he could come along on our trip." Uncle Danny forced a nervous smile. "I thought it would be fun for my favorite niece and my favorite nephew to tour the country together."

I screamed so loud that children on the rickety wooden rollercoaster covered their ears from the piercing shriek.

Baxter took his final bow and most of the audience shuffled off. A few lingered by the stage where Baxter sat with his rabbit. The kids stroked its pink ears and rubbed its twitchy nose.

Some of them were interested in the rabbit, too.

When we arrived at the stage, a tall man in a long overcoat was waving a five-dollar bill at Baxter. "And this says you can't prove it's not real magic!"

Baxter reached into his hat and pulled out a roll of money. "Very well, sir," he told the man, "our wager begins now." He took the man's fiver, added it to his roll, and tossed it back into the hat. "Dazzle me."

"I am a mentalist!" The man rubbed his temples. "I possess the power to read minds. It's a curse as much as a gift. I'm never surprised by Christmas presents, I always guess movie spoilers, and no one will play Go Fish with me. Ever."

The man proceeded to do the most mind-blowing demonstration I've ever seen. First, he instructed Baxter to pick a number, and then...well...

Here, try it yourself:

"And the number you

are left with,"

the man announced,

"is..."

The crowd gasped. A woman fainted.

"Burn him! He's a witch!" the kid with the teddy-bear shouted.

Baxter squirmed and I smiled. This vacation was looking up.

"Pay up, Mr. Wizard," the man said. "There's a corndog inside the park waiting for me to nom-nom-nom."

Baxter rubbed the bunny's head like a magic lamp capable of summoning a genie to solve this mystery. "No sir, I'm not yet ready to surrender."

"Hey!" I stepped forward. "I want in on this action."

Baxter's eyes went wide. "Bernice? I haven't seen you since — "

"Don't call me Bernice!" My eyes bulged and my face turned red. "And don't you dare mention the Vanishing Piñata incident. We don't speak of that. *Ever.*"

Everyone stepped away from me. Baxter shook his head and put his hands out in a sign of peace. "Okay. Don't hurt me. I bruise."

"I'm not here to bruise you!" I sucked in a deep cleansing breath. "I want to bet you. That you can't figure out how Mr. Mind Reader here did his thing."

Baxter shook his head. "No. I can't take your money. You're my cousin. It's against the magician's code."

Ha! Coward! He'd totally take my bet if he thought he could win. "Okay. Forget money. If you can't figure out how this magic works, you'll promise not to come on the road with Uncle Danny and me."

Baxter rubbed his chin as he considered my offer. "And if I win...?"

11

I put my hands on my hips and wiggled my head a bit. "You name it!"

"If I win," he said, "You will be my lovely magician's assistant for the rest of the summer."

"You're on!" I told him, and then I thought about it... the rest of the summer? Magician's assistant? What did that mean? It didn't matter, I had him beat.

Baxter turned to the man. "This isn't magic. It's math!"

"Math," the bratty kid chimed in. "I knew it. Witch-math!"

Baxter continued. "No matter what number you choose the answer is always 5!"

My face felt hot and red.

"The secret lies in step 3 where we add a number. You can pick any number that can be divided by 2. **The final answer will always be the number divided by 2.** In this case he asked me to add **10** to our total, hence our final answer is **5**."

Jaws dropped, people counted their fingers and went over the steps in their heads.

"Math-a-magical!" The kid whispered.

Everyone applauded.

Everyone but the man.

And me.

"It's a clever trick. Try it on your friends and pets at home tonight," Baxter told the gathered. "They'll be amazed."

"Well, you figured me out. There goes my corndog." The not-so-psychic man searched for spare change in his pockets as he sulked away. "Looks like it's cotton candy for dinner. Again."

The crowd dispersed as Baxter put his hat back on and turned to me. "Ah, Berni, my lovely assistant, your costume's backstage."

CHAPTER TWO
JACKSONVILLE, FL

And that's how I ended up inside a box, being sawed in half (or should that be "sawn"?) for the amusement of a bunch of Shriners in Florida. Not one of them was the least bit concerned for my well-being, if that gives you any indication of how convincing Baxter is as a magician.

That's the plan for the summer, it turns out. Yeah, that's right, Uncle Danny (the snake!) had it planned this way all along. You didn't think Baxter had that itchy "lovely assistant" abomination of a suit by coincidence, did you?

When the show was over, Uncle Danny collected a fat check from the Head Shriner, and Baxter stood at the front of the stage shaking hands and answering questions from guys in funny hats with tassels on them (the hats, not the guys) and their grandchildren (no tassels).

Shriners, if you don't know, are a bunch of old guys who wear funny hats and do good deeds around the world. They put on a circus and they build hospitals in places where they don't have them. They're kind of like the Boy Scouts for grampas. Plus, they ride around on tiny little cars in parades, which looks like fun. My grandpa never rode go-karts. Or trimmed his crazy eyebrows. But that's another story.

Anyway, that left me to pack up the magic show. It wasn't hard work, just a few boxes that collapsed down, and some others that filled up. All of it fit onto a little cart that made it easy to wheel everything to the Bunkmobile.

Besides, I really wasn't in the mood to talk with old dudes and kiddies. My "lovely assistant" underwear was riding up and I wanted to scratch somewhere a Lovely Assistant doesn't scratch in public.

Which is why I was hidden behind the little guillotine with the trick blade on it, sneaking in a secret scratch, when a voice came from the shadows off to the left. I pretty much jumped out of my wedgie.

"You're new to the act, aren't you?"

I turned and saw The Mustache.

There was a man behind it. He was tall and he wore a dark suit. But mostly what I saw was that magnificent mustache.

"Um, yeah," I said, distracted by his lip-warmer. He must trim it with hedge clippers. "This is my first show. I'm not really sure what I'm supposed to be doing."

The Mustache bobbed as he spoke. "Is he your cousin?"

"Yeah. How'd you know?"

"He doesn't have any reported siblings. Plus, I saw your uncle." The Mustache curled a bit at the corners. Maybe that was a smile. "And your, ah, vehicle out front."

I looked him straight in The Mustache. "What do you know about Uncle Danny?"

"What do you know about your cousin?" The Mustache asked back. "And his parents?"

Hmm. What did I know? I hadn't seen any of them in a few years. "Who are you?" I asked The Mustache.

But The Mustache had turned away, walking off. "Ask your Uncle Danny about Baxter's parents."

What about Baxter's parents?

CHAPTER THREE
PENSACOLA, FL

It was a dark and stormy night when we pulled up to the creepy haunted theater.

Well, no, not really. It was still early afternoon, and the weather was nice and balmy, with a steady breeze that kept it from getting too hot. But none of that made the handwritten sign on the front door any less goose bump-worthy.

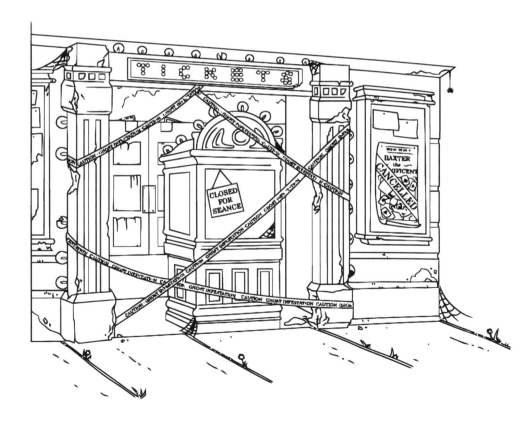

"Maybe they mean science?" I suggested. "Like a fair. With baking soda volcanoes and ribbons and poster board."

"Science isn't spelled that way, Berni," Uncle Danny said.

"I know that and you know that," I said, "but do they know that? It could be a quirk in their Southern accent. Or maybe it's an autocorrect issue. "

Uncle Danny shook his head, as he spotted a frightened man running from the lobby. "Even Science isn't that scary."

"Come on." Baxter rose, his eyes glued on the theater.

I didn't move. "You go on ahead. I'll stay here with Uncle Danny. I've been meaning to organize his 8-track collection. We'll keep the engine running. And the doors locked."

I have two dire fears — ghosts and asparagus. When I was six, I had a recurring nightmare about an aspara-ghost. *Shudder*. But given a choice between the two, I'd gladly drink an asparagus milkshake with asparagus sauce and a side of asparagus than face down a single ghost. That's fact.

"You have to come," Baxter said. "You're the Lovely Assistant."

"Throw that in my face, why don't you," I said. "Look, if you need an assist, I'll be in the car. I'll honk or something."

Baxter grabbed my arm and dragged me toward the entrance. "There's only one way to conquer your fears!"

"Hide under your bed and weep?" I asked.

Either he wasn't listening or didn't care, cause he pulled me through the empty lobby and into the back of the theater. The dimmers were set to spooky as we entered. Empty theaters are always a little creepy, but the small card table with the crystal ball setup on stage in front of the black background was ominous.

At least I didn't see any asparagus.

"I'm sorry, but no one is allowed back here until we finish the ghost-termination," a large man in a small suit said as he ushered us back toward the exit.

"Works for me. Let's run screaming back to the Bunkmobile," I said.

Baxter shot me a look. "We're the entertainment," Baxter said, turning back to the man. "I'm Baxter the Magnificent. Did you say ghost?"

The large man took our arms and turned us around. "Oliver Pork is the name. And I'd welcome you to the Pork Theater, but... yes, we have to get rid of some ghosts."

He walked us back out through the lobby and out the glass doors. "There won't be any entertaining until we can send these poltergeists packing."

"Your ghost problem is no problem," Baxter told him. "I'm a professional debunker."

"Is that so?" Mr. Pork asked. "And what does that mean? You took an online course?"

Baxter gave him a smug smile. "It means I've spent a lifetime proving that the impossible is in fact never possible."

Mr. Pork looked down at the kid in an ill-fitting tuxedo standing on the sidewalk outside his theater. "A lifetime? How old are you, again?"

"It's true!" A haggard lady charged toward us from across the street. "Ghosts do exist! I saw it with my own eyes." The lenses of her spectacles were as thick as the glass at the aquarium downtown, so take the 'my own eyes' comment with a grain of salt.

"This is Mrs. Brittlebotz," Mr. Pork said. "She lives in the apartment directly across the street."

Mrs. Brittlebotz nodded emphatically. "The ghost floats around every Monday, after midnight. I'm a night owl, myself. I can't sleep a wink. Got a case of the insomnia. So usually, I'm up late sweeping floors, vacuuming and doing my laundry. And one night while I was mopping my kitchen, I looked over in the theater's upstairs window and there it was — staring at me. Flapping in the breeze."

She pointed up at the single window high above the marquee. There was nothing there now. Thankfully.

"Today is Tuesday," Baxter observed.

"The ghost was there just last night," Mrs. Brittlebotz confirmed. "I'd finished my laundry and was doing the dishes. And there it was, flapping around. And then, poof! It's gone."

"Poof," Mr. Pork confirmed, and pulled out a phone. "Here's a picture an eye-witness took from the street."

"That's the attic," Mr. Pork said. "There's nothing in there but a bunch of old props. No one has been up there in weeks. So whatever's lurking around in that window, it's not human."

I pulled Baxter away. It was time for a sidebar. "Look, I agreed to help you with your stupid magic show. But I'm not going anywhere near this. I don't do ghosts."

"The show must go on!" Baxter said. "What if I can prove to you there's no ghost?" He made a spooky face and did a little thing with his hands. Ghost fingers.

I grabbed his hands. "I'd be pro-that. But don't squint your face like that again. Doesn't do you any favors."

Baxter spun to Mr. Pork. "Take us to the attic!"

"Us?" I asked. "As in … me? I think there's some kind of mistake."

Mr. Pork stared at Baxter like he was crazy. I was inclined to go with Mr. Pork's good judgment. "I'm not gonna let some kids go up there! Not with a ghost."

"The only way I can prove there's no ghost is by seeing this haunted attic for myself." Baxter pointed up at the window. "I'm sure you have ghost insurance or something."

Mr. Pork gave it some thought. "I don't know if we're covered for that."

"Look, if I go up there and can't prove this ghost is fake," Baxter promised, "you don't have to pay for our show tonight."

That did it. It would seem Mr. Pork was more concerned about his theater's budget than our being haunted to death, or whatever it is ghosts do. He grabbed Baxter's little hand and shook it excitedly. "Deal!"

Moments later, we stood in front of the large wooden door to the attic. Mr. Pork gave us the key, but he wouldn't even go past the second floor. Too scared. I offered to stay and comfort him, but Baxter dragged me along.

Baxter opened the door. A cloud of dust gusted out. We coughed for a bit, then focused our eyes inside. A creaky staircase led up to the dark old attic where the ghost was allegedly floating around.

The sun had started to go down and the shadows were thick as we crept up the creaky wooden stairs. I stayed uncomfortably close to Baxter. I mentally noted the boy and I should have a frank discussion about deodorant. "If an asparagus jumps out at me, I'm so going to freak."

At the top of the stairs, Baxter flipped on his flashlight. We ducked under cobwebs and breathed in thick dust. There was a lot of it, and it blew around in little clouds. Drafty, this attic. Lots of breeze. I'd bet it leaked when it rained.

Baxter aimed his flashlight at the floor. "Judging from the dust and lack of footprints, no one's been up here in a long long time."

"That's good enough for me!" I said. "Let's go back downstairs."

"No," Baxter stopped me. "What it means is, if no one was up here, what did the lady see from her apartment?"

Baxter shined the light on a clutter of props and furniture. Almost every inch of the place was filled with costume racks or a creepy mannequin or a big mirror. The breeze through here made a lot of it move. Spooky, even without ghosts.

"I don't see any ghosts," I said. "But there are some clothes here I may have nightmares about. Fashion nightmares."

Baxter turned to the large window behind us. "This must be the window where the ghost appeared." He looked through it and across the street. "And that would be Mrs. Brittleblotz's apartment."

"Think we can get out of here?" I asked. "I've seen enough. And the sun is starting to go down."

"Yes, I think we can. We have a show to prepare for." Baxter turned back toward the steps.

"What? A show?" I hurried to catch up with him. "But what about the ghost?"

"I thought it was obvious. There isn't a ghost." Baxter was running down the stairs and I charged down after him.

Baxter didn't stop running until we were in the auditorium. "Stop the séance!!" he announced, breaking the solemn silence on stage, where Mr. Pork, Mrs. Brittlebotz and a few other locals held hands at a table.

Some of the townsfolk had taken seats in the auditorium, watching the kooks on the stage. Guess you get entertainment where you can find it in these little towns.

"We are in the middle of communicating with the ghost!" Mr. Pork said.

"I'm afraid that's going to be a one-sided conversation," Baxter chimed, climbing up on the stage. "There is no ghost."

The crowd in the seats booed a little. "Down in front!" someone yelled.

Mr. Pork jumped from his seat and approached Baxter. "But what about the picture? What about Mrs. Brittlebotz?"

Baxter turned to her. "I have one question for you, madam."

Mrs. Brittlebotz nodded, uncertain.

"When," Baxter asked, "is laundry day?"

The woman looked confused. "Why, Monday, of course. That's always been laundry day."

Baxter turned to Mr. Pork. "And there you have it.".

Mr. Pork didn't make the connection. "Have what?"

"The ghost," Baxter explained, as if he was speaking to a particularly dense kindergartner, "only comes out on Monday! Laundry day!"

I have to admit, I hadn't figured it out yet, either. "Are you trying to say that the ghost likes the smell of bleach?"

Baxter sighed. "It's very simple. Mrs. Brittlebotz hangs her clothes on a line on top of her building."

Mrs. Brittlebotz nodded. "It's true. Gets a nice breeze up there."

"Indeed it does," Baxter confirmed. "Mr. Pork, you may be interested to know that, along with a bunch of old props and clothing, your attic also is host to a pretty steady wind."

"Yeah," I confirmed. "You really should look into insulating. I bet you're losing a fortune air conditioning this place."

"That wind," Baxter continued, "cuts through the room and moves certain items about. Including a large mirror."

"Eureka!" I shouted, and everyone turned to me. "I don't even know what that means, just always wanted to say it."

"The ghost you were seeing in the window," Baxter went on, "wasn't a ghost. It was Mrs. Brittlebotz's laundry. She hangs it out to dry on a line on her roof. The mirror in the attic caught a white sheet in the reflection. And then when the wind changes direction, the mirror moves away, and the ghost disappears."

They all looked amazed. I was a bit amazed myself.

"So? The show?" Baxter said. "It must go on, right?"

I moved close to Baxter's ear. "Can you prove asparagus doesn't exist? Asking for a friend."

CHAPTER FOUR
MACON, GA

"Is this your card?"

Yes, he actually said "is this your card?" I didn't know real life people actually said that.

But the audience loved it, and there was plenty of applause. We took our bows and the curtains closed.

"How'd you do that card thing?" I asked as we packed the gear away. I'd seen him prepare the giant Queen of Diamonds to be revealed at the end, so I knew it was coming. But that wasn't the impressive part. "How'd you get her to pick that card?"

"A magician," he said, "never reveals his secrets."

I raised an eyebrow at him. "Not even to his Lovely Assistant? How am I supposed to Lovely Assist if I don't know how the trick is done?"

He shook his head. "All you need to do is wave your arms and say 'tah-dah' every once in awhile. Let me handle the magic."

"Is that right?" I let the box I was holding drop to the floor. Loudly. "Then I'll leave the clean-up to you, too, Mr. Magic-Pants."

I stormed out, paying no attention to his protests. Time for me to get out of this itchy outfit.

While I had planned to step into the Bunkmobile to do just that, instead I stepped into Uncle Danny's favorite coffee mug.

I heard someone yell "Fore!", and a purple golf ball bounced off the wall next to me.

"Sorry," Uncle Danny said. "You threw off my aim."

"Is this all you do while we're on stage?" I asked him. "No wonder this place is such a mess!"

"You call it a mess," Uncle Danny lined up a putt. "I call it a course with challenging hazards." He let his club fly, and the ball bounced over an empty pizza box, rebounded off the rabbit's cage, and rolled into his coffee mug.

"Not bad," I told him, taking the club. "But watch this." I eyed the course, charted my route, then knocked the ball off the leg of the table, off a half-filled soda bottle, and into an overturned Styrofoam cup.

Uncle Danny nodded, impressed. "Your talents are wasted in the Lovely Assistance field."

"You can say that again." I picked up the ball and tossed it to him. "I need to do something about that."

Uncle Danny caught the ball. "You gonna take over the top spot? I don't know if you're cut out for the whole top hat thing." He dropped the ball and said, "Eight ball, corner pocket."

"Wrong game," I told him, but then he knocked the golf ball into the pocket of a pair of cargo shorts he'd left in the far corner. Say what you will about Uncle Danny, but the man's got a sense of humor.

My turn. "I don't want to be a magician," I told him. "But I'm sick of being his rabbit-fetcher."

"Maybe you should talk with him about some changes," Uncle Danny suggested, as I lined up a seven-foot putt into the back bedroom, off the bathroom's accordion-style door, and into one of Uncle Danny's sneakers. "I bet he'd be reasonable about it," Uncle Danny added, revealing just how little he knew about my cousin in less than ten words.

I gave the ball a tap, and it rolled true for half the hallway, then caught some rough on a worn spot on the fake-grass carpet and I had to one-putt it from the foot of Uncle Danny's bed, around a still-sticky ice cream sandwich wrapper he'd left there the night before. Tricky shot, but a birdie all the same.

"You're right," I told Uncle Danny, which is not a phrase I used with him often. "I need to make some changes."

"Uh, what I said," corrected Uncle Danny, "was that you should talk to him."

I nodded, handing him the putter. "Oh, I'm sure he'll have plenty to say."

CHAPTER FIVE

MOBILE, AL

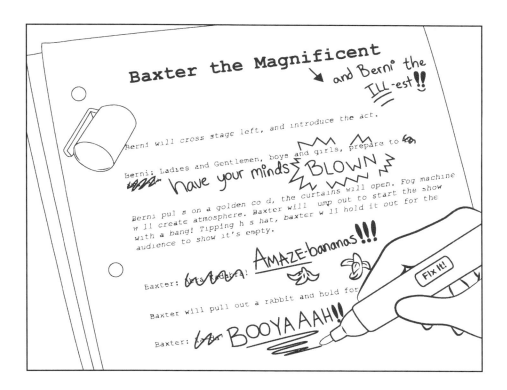

"This is sabotage!" Baxter fumed as the curtain closed.

"I thought the routine needed some punch-ups," I said to the irate boy magician. "I just adjusted the dialogue so I'd be more comfortable. Not everyone can say 'Presto-Change-o' without giggling."

I guess the spirit of creativity and invention had gotten the best of me, and I made a few small enhancements to the Baxter The Magnificent experience.

But Baxter wasn't feeling it. "It's not dialogue, it's 'patter'. Everything a magician says or does is for a specific reason. You can't say 'Boo-ya' after every trick!"

He gave me a once over. "And what happened to your costume?"

"Updated. The old one was OLD. This is what today's Lovely Assistant is wearing." I did a twirl to model my new look. "Besides, the old one made me itch. I think I'm allergic to it. Or the rabbit. Or you." I stuck my tongue out. "And Boo-yah is staying."

Uncle Danny poked his head in, his arms filled with bags of wacky inventions. "Hey, Baxter, do you think I could borrow a few sheckles from your piggy-bank?"

Baxter's eyes blazed. "No one touches my piggy-bank!" It's where he kept his money when it wasn't in his hat.

"But there's something we have to buy!" Uncle Danny complained. "It might make the Bunkmobile extinct!"

We followed Uncle Danny out to the showroom floor. Booths and tables were set up in the cavernous convention hall. Inventors shouted like carnival barkers trying to wave you over to take a look at their creations.

But Uncle Danny had eyes for only one of them.

"Ladies and gents. How would you like to surf the waves of Hawaii in the morning and ski the snowy Alps in the afternoon? What if you could get your kids to soccer practice without ever leaving your couch? Imagine sleeping in late and skipping the school bus, but still being the first one to arrive at school!"

People nodded in the audience. Except for Baxter, who scowled. Or at least I think he scowled. Scowling was his default look.

"Teleportation!" said the man on the stage, as excited as if he'd been saying "Free Ice Cream!" "You've seen it in the movies, heard it talked about in science fiction novels and comic-book conventions."

"Balderdash," Baxter muttered, and I made a mental note to come up with a list of things he could say that wouldn't make him sound like he came from a century when stage magicians still mattered.

The man on the stage went on. "Well, tomorrow is today. Meet the Port-a-Porter! The very first teleportation machine designed for home use."

People gasped and took pictures. A few went for their wallets.

The man paced. "The Port-a-Porter will revolutionize how we travel. How we ship Christmas packages. How we get pizza delivered to our homes!"

"Woooooooo," said the crowd.

"And it's not just for deliveries. The Port-a-Porter works on people, too! Make motion sickness a thing of the past as you disintegrate and molecularly reboot in the blink of an eye! No more filling up the car with gas. Skip the lines at the airport. Or just use it to magically appear behind your annoying sister and scare the snot out of her!" He waved his hands at the cardboard box. "This is your chance! For just $19.99, I'll give you this entire instruction manual on how to build your own Port-a-Porter and you can have the joys of teleportation in your own home!"

The idea of teleporting Baxter somewhere far, far away held a certain appeal to me, I'll admit.

"This contraption could put you out of business," I said to Baxter. "This is 'now you see it, now you don't' for real."

"Hmph," Baxter hmphed.

"Who wants to give it a go?!" the man on the stage called out.

People surged forward, raising their hands, apparently discounting the potential side-effects of molecular disintegration. Uncle Danny hooted and waved his arms, hoping to get the man's attention.

The sales guy looked right past him to a girl with her red hair pulled back in a bow and the cutest sneakers.

He invited her on the stage.

At this point I started taking pictures with my phone. If a miracle was about to happen, it was my civic duty to post pictures on social media. Besides, I really liked her shoes.

"Hello, Penny," the man said, reading the name off her convention badge. "Thanks for volunteering. If you would just step inside the Port-a-Porter." He escorted Penny inside the machine and shut the aluminum foil door. "Don't worry, this won't hurt a bit."

"Ooookay," her tiny voice came from inside, and there were some laughs in the audience.

"And now. Sit back and watch THE FUTURE." He hit a small CD player which blasted out some dramatic music. "Count with me — Five. Four..."

The crowd joined in, "...Three. Two. One!"

Then nothing. No flash. No laser beams. No explosion. The crowd went silent. This thing was looking like a port-a-dud.

"Aaaaaah!" A shrill scream roared out from behind us.

Everyone turned to see Penny standing far from the Port-a-Porter, entirely freaked out from her unbelievable journey.

"Booyah!" the man on the stage said. I nudged Baxter in a 'toldya so' way, as the man opened the door of the Port-a-Porter to reveal it completely empty.

She'd done it. She really teleported. I'd never be late for school again!

People stormed the stage, waving money at the man.

Uncle Danny grabbed his wallet. "Do either of you have five dollars? I only have fifteen. Hurry! Before it sells out!"

Baxter folded his arms. "It's not worth it."

"Not worth it?! Didn't you hear what he said about pizza delivery?"

"He didn't teleport anyone. It's all a fake-out to get your money. A trick. You just need to examine the pictures to know how he did it. There are three things in the pictures that will tell you what's up."

Hmf. This seemed impossible. So I went to my phone and pulled up the pictures, side by side.

"So, how did he do it?" I asked Baxter. "How did Penny appear all the way behind us in the blink of an eye?"

"She didn't," Baxter explained. "But her sister did."

"Twins!" I said.

Baxter nodded. "There are two clues in the last picture. The girl who appeared behind us is identical except for two small details. Can you see them?"

I scanned the picture.

"Look at her hair," he prompted.

"The bow," I realized, "there are no dots on it!"

"Right," Baxter said. "There's one more difference."

"The name on her badge," I saw. "It says 'Peggy Adams' not 'Penny'."

"Twins names," Baxter confirmed. "Peggy and Penny. And they have different shoes."

"But what happened to Penny? Last we saw her she was in the Port-a-Porter." I paused at the horrific thought. "Was she disintegrated?"

Baxter rolled his eyes. "Of course not. Look at the last picture of the empty box. Do you see anything that looks familiar?"

That's when I saw them. "The shoes! It's Penny!"

"Right," Baxter said. "There must have been a disguise hidden inside the cardboard box. When we all turned to look at the girl we thought was Penny, she slipped out into the crowd in disguise. "

"Aha!" I shouted, getting it. "When Penny... err... Peggy... screamed from behind us. No one was looking."

"Misdirection. The magician's best friend." Baxter stepped in front of the salesman and raised his hands to get everyone's attention. "Ladies and gentleman, before you spend your hard-earned money, I should inform you this girl did not teleport. The demonstration was a trick."

I whipped Penny's hoodie back to reveal the disappeared twin.

"Boo-yaah!"

Then I whispered to her, "Love your shoes."

CHAPTER SIX
HIGHWAY I-10,
HEADING WEST

As we drove toward our gig at a Biloxi Auto Show, Baxter
ran through a final check of all his props. A stickler for
organization, our Baxter, and everything had its place — the
sponge balls, the cups and balls, the cards, the jumbo cards,
the scarves, the four trick wands, the straitjacket, the shackles,
etc, etc.

Last but not least, Baxter pulled his rabbit out of the hat to put it back into its cage. (In case you were wondering, the rabbit's name is Warren... get it?) While his back was turned, I picked up the hat and felt around in it. I found no pockets, and no hidden compartments.

"Never touch that!" Baxter snatched the hat away. "The bond between a magician and his top hat is sacred!"

Far be it from me to stand between a boy and his hat. "But where does the rabbit go? How do you do it?"

"A magician never reveals his secrets," he sniffed. He pulled a wad of money from the hat. He kept it in there for his mysterious "wagers." He put the cash into his corny pink piggy-bank.

"You didn't seem to have any trouble revealing Mr. Port-a-Porter's secret yesterday," I reminded him.

Baxter tucked his top hat into its special, silk-lined box. "That man wasn't a magician," he said. "He was a charlatan."

"His name was Charlotte? Kinda girly for a salesman."

"It's not a name. A charlatan is not a magician," he explained, and he was in full-blown lecture mode now. "They try to fool people."

"Isn't that what magicians do?"

"Only for fun. I —" He stopped, then corrected himself, "— we are entertainers. Magicians have an unspoken contract with our audience to provide them with good, wholesome fun. Like actors on television. Actors are not really the characters they portray, but they're not trying to trick you into believing they are. You know they're just pretending. Magicians are just pretending."

I nodded. He seemed to take this charlatan thing mighty seriously.

"Typically, a charlatan isn't just lying to you, he's after something. Usually money." Baxter pointed to a taped-up poster on the wall of Harry Houdini wrapped in cuffs. "Because we know all the tricks, magicians feel a special responsibility to 'debunk' charlatans. Harry Houdini was known for it. My parents have even consulted with the FBI on some cases."

His parents. I remembered The Mustache a couple states back and thought I should make a note to talk to Uncle Danny about Baxter's parents. I brought up my phone and began to type a memo.

"Give me that." Baxter snatched the phone away.

"Hey!" I reached for it, but he pulled it away. "Didn't anyone ever teach you, you never take a phone away from a sixth-grade girl!"

"One moment, please. I'm demonstrating." He placed the phone on the table and produced a big, red handkerchief from his sleeve, waving it around in the air.

"Be careful with that," I said, choking up with emotion, "It's my best friend."

Baxter wrapped the handkerchief around the phone.

My precious phone. I can't stress this enough.

"Pay attention," he said, and lifted a big hammer. He held it by the head, then flipped it around in the air and caught it by the handle. Kind of mesmerizing, seeing it flip like that, but it was right over my phone and I didn't like where this was going.

"Watch closely," he said.

He slammed the hammer down on the phone.

I gasped. My phone! My lifeline. My rock.

I don't really know what happened next, but I do remember that my face was red-hot and I was on top of Baxter on the floor, shaking him and saying, "What? Is? Your? Problem?"

"Hey!" Uncle Danny called from the driver's seat up front. "What are you kids doing back there?"

"Just some magic," Baxter assured him. "Keep your eyes on the road!"

Baxter squirmed out from under me and crawled around the table.

"Now a charlatan," he said as I chased him after him, "would say that the phone was gone, and you are fresh out of luck, and maybe you should buy a new one from him."

"You're the one who is going to be fresh out of luck!" I said, snatching his ankle with two hands.

He turned around, fear in his eyes. "But a magician would say...is that a ring-tone?"

The dull chime of a ringing phone filled my ears. My phone! I looked down and could see its bedazzled skin peeking out of my pants pocket.

I ripped it out. The call was coming from "BAXTER THE MAGNIFICIENT."

Baxter pulled the handkerchief through his fist, and it turned into a bouquet of plastic flowers. "Magic." He forced a sheepish smile.

CHAPTER SEVEN
JACKSON, MI

The audience was named Myrtle. She ate macaroni salad out of a plastic container and slurped from a juice box (prune, I might add). Her park-issued broom and dustpan leaned on the empty chair beside her.

Even Uncle Danny was a no-show, and he was part of this ridiculous Abracadabra-athon.

A monotone woman's voice crackled over the park loudspeaker — "ATTENTION, MR. MERMAID'S SPLASH-A-GEDDON WATERPARK AND PETTING ZOO EMPLOYEES."

Myrtle froze, balancing a spoonful of wobbling pasta before her wide-open mouth, as if she couldn't chew and listen at the same time.

The voice on the speaker droned on,"MR. MERMAID'S SPLASH-O-RAMA WATER PARK AND PETTING ZOO WILL BE CLOSING IN FIVE MINUTES DUE TO ZERO ATTENDANCE. THANK YOU AND GET OUT."

Myrtle was already hobbling toward the exit.

And so was Baxter.

Magicians. Always vanishing when you need them.

I was stuck levitating ten feet above the stage.

(I could tell you how it's done, but then I'd have to kill you.)

(Actually, I couldn't really tell you, and even if I could, Baxter would kill me.)

I carefully climbed back to safe ground and headed to the park entrance. My nasal passages were assaulted with a stink that reminded me of the smell of the fish pier down the local shore. Voices in unison chanted in the distance. "FISH! FISH! FISH ARE PEOPLE TOO! FISH! FISH! FISH ARE PEOPLE TOO!"

A mob of reporters surrounded four odd people marching in a circle outside the entrance gates.

The leader of the quartet shouted through a bullhorn, "We, the mer-people of the world, demand justice! We want this offensive water park to turn off the water!"

His crew let out a cheer and shouted a few "amens."

"Hold up." I waved my hands. "You're saying you're a for reals mermaid?"

"No, young madam." He put me in the crosshairs of his bullhorn. "Mermaids are female. I am a Mer...butler."

Yes, he really said "mer-butler."

"Poppycock!" Baxter cried out. I really needed to sign the boy up for an online course on modern slang.

Baxter went toe to toe...err...fin?...with the mega-phone wielding protestor. "There are no such things as Mermaids...or uh...Mer-Butlers. They are a myth."

"I'm afraid you are myth-taken," the man spat through the mega-phone. "Myth-ter...?"

"Mr. Bunkhouse. Baxter Bunkhouse. Conjurer extraordinaire and professional debunker."

"Woooooooooooooooo," said the crowd.

Actually, it was just me. I drew a few strange stares.

"And you are?" Baxter asked the man.

"My name is Larry Lumpowitz. Owner and proprietor of the new Mermania Water Park and Paintball. The only officially sanctioned Merfolk park from the water-breathers union of America."

"You don't even have fins," Baxter said.

"How rude of you, young sir. I was mocked in fish school. Does the bullying ever end?" Larry cast an accusing eye at Baxter.

Baxter crossed his arms. "What proof do you even have you're a mermaid? How do we know you're not here trying to promote your own water park?"

The reporters stuck out their voice recorders and microphones to capture the Larry's response.

"Well, I smell like a fish." He sniffed his armpits in demonstration and invited the gathered mob to have a whiff.

"That doesn't prove anything," I said. "If fishy-smells make you a mermaid, Baxter's underwear is Poseidon."

Larry frowned. "What if I breathed underwater?"

"Wooooooooooooo," said the crowd. Not just me this time.

Baxter rubbed his chin. "If you can hold your breath underwater for say...ten minutes...I think it would be sufficient evidence."

Larry smiled. "Okay. But if I can do that, this park will be forced to shut down!"

Reporters nodded. Baxter shrugged.

"To the pool!" Larry shouted.

As the sun dipped beneath the Towering Splashferno waterslide, we gathered around the edges. Larry and his entourage stood at the ramp on the shallow end. Larry adjusted his big, squid-shaped bowtie. "Today," he announced, "I will prove I am a Mer-Butler!"

"Even holding one's breath for a few minutes requires intense physical preparation. And an athletic physique." Baxter eyed the Lumpowitz's sagging belly.

"If you wish, you can keep track of the time." Larry offered Baxter his wristwatch."

"I do wish." Baxter held up his own stopwatch. "But I prefer to use my own precision verified timepiece."

"How do we know you're not hiding a big-old oxygen thing-a-magigees under that suit?" I asked.

The tuxedoed man opened his jacket and turned in a circle. "Feel free to search," he said.

"I think we can take your word for that," I said. The way his belly strained his buttons, we'd be able to tell.

Larry stopped dramatically by the edge of the pool. "Kids, what you are about to see should only be attempted by a professional mermaid. Do not try it at home."

He dangled a foot over the water and held his nose. "One small step for Mer-Man," the words came out nasally. "One large splash for Mer-kind."

Followed by his mer-friends, Larry waded into the water, first over his ankles, then his knees, then up to his waist.

One of his buddies handed Larry a plastic-coated sign, and he stood, his back to us, head under water. Larry held the sign over his head.

Baxter squeezed the stopwatch in his right palm, starting the timer.

"He seems confident," I said.

"Con-men usually are, hence the 'con,' otherwise they'd just be men." He glanced at the timer. "One minute down."

Three minutes passed, then four, then five.

As a spectator sport, breath-holding makes watching paint dry seem exciting. To pass the time, I decided to give it a go. I gulped a mouthful of air, puffed my cheeks, held my breath and counted in my head.

One Mississippi.
Two Mississippi.
Three Mississippi.

I got fifteen Mississippis before I spit out my air (and my gum, sorry lady with the blue hat and sunglasses, hope you didn't have to cut too much of your hair to remove that chewed up wad).

Uncle Danny showed up. He was wearing a snorkel and mask, and carrying his flippers. "Did I miss anything? I fell asleep in the kiddie pool."

Ten minutes passed.

"Fish breathe under water," I said. "Maybe he's hiding gills."

Baxter narrowed his eyes on Larry. "He's hiding something," Baxter said. "But it's not gills."

"Twenty minutes!" A photographer shouted. "Amazing!"

Applause erupted from the assembled.

Still underwater, Larry turned, and walked towards us. His head emerged from the water with a cocky grin. He climbed out of the pool to cheers and slaps on his water-logged back. "Fish-man for the win! Now, who's ready to close this joint down?"

Baxter scanned the water. The pool was clear enough to see to the bottom. There was nothing down there. No secret oxygen tank or any magic-gimmick.

Larry smirked. "Well, my debunker friend, do you plan to apologize to my mer-folk brethren?"

Baxter shook his head. "It's you who should be sorry. For you, Larry Lumpowitz, are no Mermaid or a Mer-butler. You're, in fact, a Mer-FRAUD!!"

Baxter had that gleam in his eye, which usually meant he was on to something.

What do you think? Was there something fishy going on? Well, more fishy? Fishy-er?

I'll give you a second to review the facts.

And in the meantime, I'll leave you with this key piece of evidence —

Woops! My bad. Wrong picture.

I meant this...

Baxter turned to me. "Remember, everything about a magician has meaning. What do we see out of the ordinary?"

I looked at Larry and sighed. "Where to start? That tuxedo needs to be put back in Davy Jones' Locker and buried deep, deep, deep beneath the sea." I shuddered trying to erase the fashion faux paus from the browser history of my mind.

"Only a complete weirdo would wear something like that at a water park," I said, giving Baxter's tux the once over.

"Mine's kind of a magician dress code thing." He pinched lint off his lapel.

"At least you don't wear that ridiculous oversized bow-tie," I said. "It doesn't even match."

"Eureka! That's a clue," Baxter said. "And then there's the sign he held above his head. It's no mere slogan, it's a tip-off."

"Exactly what I was thinking," I lied.

"How does a man breathe underwater without an oxygen tank?" Baxter questioned. "The answer is right in front of our faces—""

He turned to Uncle Danny, who was picking his nose. He had a "deer in the headlights" look. He stared at us dumbly through his scuba mask.

A gasp went up amongst the crowd.

Uncle Danny hid the offending finger behind his back. "It was just an itch, not a pick."

"The snorkel!" Baxter shouted.

Baxter marched over to Larry and tore the bow tie from his neck.

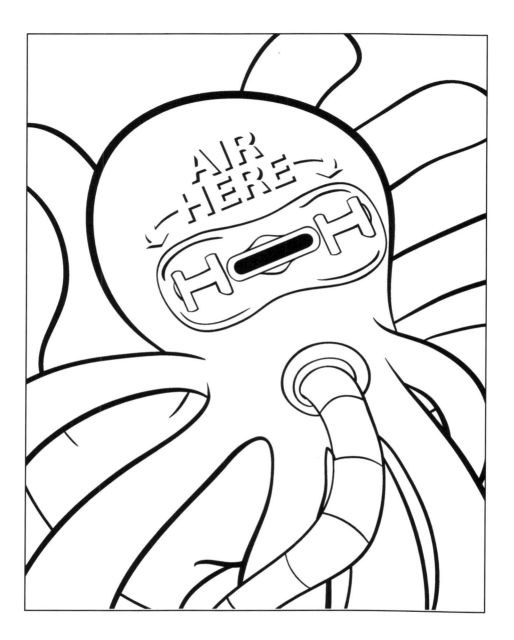

"He was breathing underwater through a snorkel hidden
behind his bow-tie which ran through his sleeve and up his arm!"

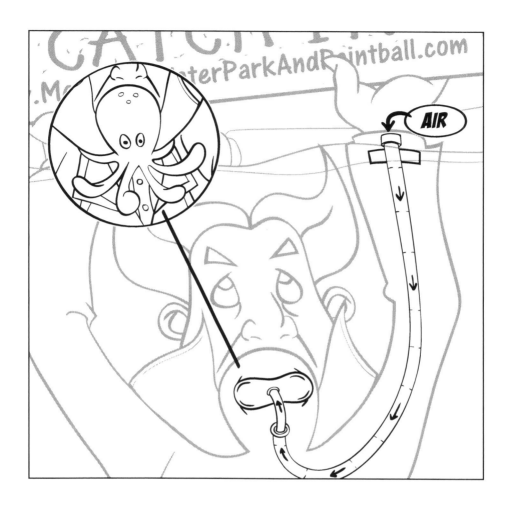

"Okay! You got me." Larry threw down his protest sign."I can't believe I wore the fish perfume for nothing! I'm breaking out in hives!" He stormed out, scratching his armpits.

Baxter took center stage in front of the reporters who nodded, jotted notes and snapped pictures. "Ladies and gentle-reporters, the park will re-open in ten minutes. And, today only, Baxter the Magnificent will be performing in the Titanic Deck amphitheater."

"Wear your life-preservers," I added.

CHAPTER EIGHT
I-10 WESTBOUND AT NIGHT

Could you sleep with that snoring?

We had to be at our next show early in the morning, so Uncle Danny was driving at night. I decided to sit up front with him.

He wore glasses when he drove in the dark, which reminded me of my father. And my father looks a little like Baxter's father, so I remembered Baxter's parents. And what The Mustache told me to ask Uncle Danny.

So I did.

"What's the deal with Baxter's parents?"

"Huh?" Uncle Danny had been focusing intently on the road, but this caught his attention. "What do you mean?"

"Where's Uncle Manny? And Aunt Winnie? How come Baxter's with us?"

"I told you. They've got something going on and needed me to take him."

"But what do they have going on?" I asked. "Are they in trouble?"

"What?" Uncle Danny looked at me, then back at the road. "No. They're in California."

"California, huh?"

"They've been performing out there. That's really the whole point of this trip. We're going to see them," Uncle Danny went on, getting into it. "They're doing shows at this place called the Magician's Palace."

"The Magician's Palace!" Now I was getting excited. "Where the Secret Order of Magic meets?"

Uncle Danny looked at me funny, and for a little longer than someone driving should. "What do you know about the Magician's Palace?"

"It's only the most amazing showcase for magical entertainment in the world!" I told him. "It's a members-only club, very exclusive! All the best magicians are in it, and you can't get in without an invitation from one of the members!"

"You don't care about magic," Uncle Danny said. "How do you know about this?"

I smiled. "Because Jackson Plateau is a member!"

"Who's Jackie Pluto?" Uncle Danny asked.

"Jackson Plateau!" I corrected him. "Don't you watch any TV?"

"Sports," he responded. "Do sports count? Does he play for the Giants?"

"Jackson Plateau's the star of *He Who Dealt It*." I waited, but that got no reaction from Uncle Danny. "You know the show about the guys who play cards and get into trouble with their girlfriends? It's just the number one show on television!" For a guy who doesn't have a regular job, it's a little surprising how little Uncle Danny knows about TV.

Uncle Danny nodded. "And he's a magician, is he?"

"He's an actor," I told him, and I might've rolled my eyes just a little. "But they use cards on the show, so they pass the time learning tricks, and he got accepted into the Magician's Palace!"

"How do you know all this?" Uncle Danny asked.

I huffed at him. "Don't tell me you don't remember 'Bobby Popcorn, NYPD!'"

Uncle Danny thought a second. "Wait, I know that one... something about a kid who's a police detective?"

"That was Jackson Plateau," I told him. "He played a super-smart kid who finished law school before most people started high school. But no law firm would hire him, so he worked for the police department in New York."

"Oh, right," Uncle Danny nodded. "And now he's grown up and works at the magic place?"

"He runs it now! He's president!"

I worry about Uncle Danny. It's like he's got better things to do than keep up with popular culture. Wasting his life away.

CHAPTER NINE
BATON ROUGE, LA

What do you get grandpa for his one hundredth birthday?

Apparently, a big-eared, humorless boy magician and his amazeballs lovely assistant. This gig was mostly walk-around work. That's magician-speak for 'too cheap for a stage.' Basically it means going table-to-table vanishing birthday cake without a fork.

The Birthday Boy's name was Elmer. I know this because Baxter and I were supposed to lead the Happy Birthday Song when the cake arrived. Baxter wasn't thrilled — his showmanship doesn't extend to serenading the elderly — but I was looking forward to it. I love to sing, and this is one song I know all the words to.

I don't know if you've ever seen 100 candles on a birthday cake, but it takes a blowtorch to light them. When it was carried out, I sucked in a breath to sing and took a step back for safety (my costume is totes flammable).

And then the shouting began.

"That's the man!" The old lady pointed a crooked finger right at old Elmer. Probably. Hard to tell for sure. Her finger was pretty crooked. "He's the one that kidnapped my Jimmi-HoTep!"

"What's her Jimmi-HoTep?" I asked.

"A famous Egyptian mummy that was loaned to a nearby museum in the last century," Baxter explained, because *of course* he'd know that. "It went missing and was never found!"

"Oh, not this again," came a voice from behind us. There on the other side of the flaming cake was Birthday-Boy Elmer, hands on his head. "This crazy dame keeps trying to accuse me of the mummy-napping because I was at the museum that night."

"What were you doing at a museum at night?" I asked.

"I was the groundskeeper," he said, barely keeping the candles from sizzling off what was left of his hair. "I was looking for the shovel I lost there."

"The shovel he used to break the window!" the old woman shouted, pointing again, and looking pretty pleased with herself when she saw the TV cameras caught it.

"What's with the camera?" I asked, expecting know-it-all Baxter to pipe up. Instead, this man-mountain was the one who answered.

"They're with me," he said.

I AM...
VINNIE VISION,
EXTRA LARGE MEDIUM!!

"Vinnie Vision: Extra Large Medium at Large!" Vinnie announced, and waited for applause. None came. "Sundays at seven, check your local listings."

"*You* have a TV show?" I asked. They'll let anybody in front of a camera these days.

Vinnie ignored my comment and continued. "In this thrilling episode we've re-opened a cold case of a Mummy stolen from a museum fifty years ago. My psychic investigation has brought me here, to this unassuming birthday party."

"You're not getting any cake," old Elmer grumbled.

"Psychic vibes from the other side have guided me to this culprit." Vinnie pointed at Elmer. "Officer Waldo, arrest this man!"

"Aw, fooey," Elmer told him.

This sweet old guy was no mummy-snatcher. Plus, all his candles were going to burn down and get wax all over his cake.

Baxter stepped in front of Elmer. "Nobody's arresting anybody. Psychic testimony is not permissible in a court of law. You need real evidence."

The cameras swung to Baxter, as did Vinnie's eyes. "What do you know?" Vinnie asked. "Are you gifted with the Second Sight?"

"Not second sight," Baxter shot back. "I just look twice and collect the evidence."

"Ah! A skeptic in our midst." Vinnie looked right into one of the cameras. "If you had watched the highly Extra Large Medium At Large Season 1 — now on DVD and Blu-Ray —

you would know I don't provide actual evidence. I merely point law enforcement where to look. And today I'm pointing right there." Again, Vinnie aimed his accusing finger at Elmer. Really, how many times were they going to do the finger-point thing?

Officer Waldo stepped forward. "On the other hand, I do provide evidence." He pulled some papers out of a pouch that didn't look like it belonged on a police uniform. I bet the whole get-up was a rental. "These photos show the original crime scene."

Vinnie stepped forward. "What's more, we have testimony from the only witness to the crime — security guard Janet Poodlepot!"

The old woman in the scooter putted forward. Miss Poodlepot was as old as Elmer, maybe older.

"He's the man," she declared. "I'd know that shovel-slinger anywhere!"

"Dun-dun-DUN," Vince boomed, imitating a melodramatic TV soundtrack between cupped hands. "Miss Poodlepot, can you tell us exactly what happened that night?"

"I remember it as clear as day. I was making my rounds when suddenly — POOF! — the power went out in the entire museum. Everything went dark. I heard a crash from the Egyptology exhibit. That's where Jimmi slept."

"Slept?" Baxter said.

"Jimmi?" I said. This sounded weird.

"The Mummy of Jimmi-HoTep," Vinnie clarified.

"When I entered the room, the first thing I saw was the broken window," Miss Poodlepot said. "I knew something was up. When I turned around, I saw a face! A face I'll never forget! That face!"

She pointed at Elmer.

"We've already got the finger-point shot," Vinnie told her. "Just give us the story."

Poodlepot continued. "He broke one of the three precious Egyptian vases over my head. That's the last thing I remember."

Officer Waldo jumped in to finish the story. "Miss Poodlepot was discovered on the floor the next morning, along with this man's shovel by the window!" Waldo looked like he wanted to point, but held off.

"And this evidence, along with my extra-cool-extra-sensory perception," Vinnie added, "is enough to ensure this birthday boy is going to be eating his cake behind bars."

Officer Waldo pulled out some handcuffs that definitely looked official.

"Wait!" Baxter said. "The Extra Large Medium is extra large wrong on this one! And I can prove it."

"I doubt that," Vinnie said, then turned to the cameras. "And if he can, we can edit it out right?"

"Baxter, are you sure about this one?" I asked. "You weren't even there!"

"Oh, I'm sure. It's all in the crime scene photos." Baxter exclaimed. "Have another look."

They gathered around the photos, taking a second look. So did I. Hmmmm....

I didn't see anything all that telling. I was worried for Elmer and for us. The candles were full inferno now, and the smoke alarm was going to be triggered if we didn't get to the bottom of this soon.

Baxter paced. "Miss Poodlepot said the power went out, along with all the lights."

"To bypass the alarm of course," Vinnie said. "Cunning."

Baxter shook his head. "Look at the picture of Miss Poodlepot, again. If the lights were out and it was pitch-dark throughout the museum, why was Miss Poodlepot's flashlight still on her belt?"

"Good point," I said. "And if she wasn't holding her flashlight, how could she see Elmer's face in the dark?"

"The moon was bright that night. Clear as glass!" Poodlepot shouted from her scooter.

"We'll get to the glass," Baxter told her. "But first, she said she was hit with one of the three vases. Yet look at those pictures. There's no sign of a broken vase. Each of the vases in the photo is still on its pedestal."

"Well, maybe the criminal brought his own Egyptian vase to hit her with and then cleaned up the mess." Vinnie was getting nervous. "A tidy thief. Cunning and tidy."

"You forgot to mention ridiculous," I added to his list.

"Ah! But then we get to the glass," Baxter said. "The window!"

"Yes! Proof of the break in," Vinnie added.

"Look again at the photo," Baxter said. "There's no broken glass inside the room, as it would be if the glass was broken from the outside. If you break a window from the inside, the glass falls out!"

"A break out?" I asked.

"More likely, Miss Poodlepot staged the robbery after she took the mummy herself. Broke the window and planted the stolen shovel as false evidence."

Elmer gasped. "That was my favorite shovel!"

Baxter walked to Miss Poodlepot's scooter and looked at her. "Judging from her familiarity with the mummy..."

"That's right," I nodded. "She called it by its first name!"

"...and her Egyptian-styled jewelry, I'd say you could probably find the mummy at her house. Attic or basement?" Baxter nodded, thoughtfully. "Walk-in basement, I'd say. Hard to get up into the attic on a scooter."

Miss Poodlepot's scooter suddenly jumped into gear. She nearly ran Baxter over as she raced away. "Run for it, psychic boy! The jig is up! They know! They know!"

Vinnie slashed a hand in front of his throat. "Cut! We have to burn this tape!"

"We don't use tape," the confused camera man said. "It's on a hard-drive."

I stepped in front of the camera. "No one's turning that off just yet!"

Then I cleared my throat. It was time to sing!

CHAPTER TEN
GERTIE'S "OL' FASHION" GAS-N-GRUB

I love my parents. I do.

But when I'm away from them, I also kind of love that, too.

So, yeah, we'd talked, but it wasn't a daily thing. They're having fun in Hawaii, I'm having "fun" being a Lovely Assistant, and we can talk about it every few days. No homesickness. No big thing.

Baxter, not so much. The boy talks to his parents every day, and he gets nervous if he misses a call.

Thing is, he's not much of a cell phone guy. He likes to have a big old receiver to press against his jug-ears, and buttons to punch, and a cord he can see go into a phone and across the country.

Oh, he has a celly — he's not a complete lunatic. But he says it's only for emergencies. I'm cool with that, because I'm not all that keen to call him anyway.

So every night when we stop for dinner, Baxter finds a payphone. They don't have them just anywhere these days, but there's a chain of truck stops called Gertie's "Ol' Fashion" Gas-N-Grub that always has them, along with showers for the truckers, an overnight parking area, and a restaurant.

The waitress with the big hair and the cat-eye glasses brought me my Patty Melt with cheese fries, and Uncle Danny got his Three-Bean Chili with extra beans (glad the Bunkmobile has windows!) and she put down Baxter's Garden Salad with dressing on the side (he even eats like a rabbit).

Baxter wasn't there to take his food. His seat in the booth was taken up by nothing but that silly piggy-bank. He was busy finding that payphone.

We didn't wait.

Uncle Danny mopped up the last of his chili with some cornbread when Baxter returned.

"Great news!" Baxter announced. I'd never seen him smiling so big.

"You got your money back from the payphone?" Uncle Danny asked.

"Guess who's performing at the Magician's Palace?" Baxter said.

"Your parents," I said. "We know."

"Not just my parents. Me. I'm going to be their opening act that last night!"

It was hard not to give him a smart-alecky answer, but I was busy dreaming about what it would be like to be on stage in front of Jackson Plateau.

"That's right," my cousin said. "Baxter the Magnificent will finally be making his debut at the Magician's Palace!"

I waited a moment, but he didn't say anything. So I prompted him. "And his Lovely Assistant...?"

Baxter's eyes darted away and quickly changed the subject. "Mmmm. Are those lima beans?"

It was all I could do not to launch a cheese fry at him.

"They see promise in what I've been doing," Baxter said. "Apparently, there's been a scout following our show and watching."

Hmmm. I thought. The Mustache!

I couldn't contain myself anymore. "Is Jackson Plateau going to be there?"

"Of course he is," Baxter said, cutting his carrots. "He's the current Magician's Palace President. So what?"

"I'm actually a ginormous Jackson Plateau fan. Huge. The huge-est. Not of the magic-stuff. He's an actor on TV."

"I'm aware of his lesser hobbies," Baxter nodded. "Acting. Line-dancing. Ice sculpture."

I gasped. "Lesser hobbies? It's the biggest, funniest show on TV. And he's the coolest actor on it."

Baxter went back to his salad. "Do you have a point, Berni?"

"Well," I said, "I was just thinking maybe I could do something more in the show. I took dance in the fifth grade. I was good before they kicked me out." I fired off a quick tap step with some Jazz hands to jazz it up.

"Stop," Baxter commanded. "Only magicians are allowed inside the Palace."

"Well, sure," I said. "And their Lovely Assistants."

"Only," he repeated, very clearly, so that I could have no chance to misunderstand, "magicians. You're not allowed in the Palace, Berni."

My mouth was dry. I licked my lips. "But... how can you do your show without me?"

"I somehow managed before you came along," Baxter said.

"What if I did a trick?" I was getting desperate. "You could teach me."

"Teach you?" Baxter laughed. "Berni, what I do is a respected art form, part of a long tradition, centuries old. A magician's assistant doesn't just jump in front of everyone and do some trick for the first time in front of the Secret Order of Magicians. That's ridiculous. You'd be a complete embarrassment."

Turns out, my love for cheese-fries has its limit.

CHAPTER ELEVEN
BOGGY CREEK, TX

The entire county had suffered through the worst drought in history. Zero rainfall in three months. Here's what the greatest white water rapids south of the Adirondacks looked like when we arrived:

Cookie Scout Troup 71 set out for a weekend of white water rafting. Without any 'white water' to be found, the Cookie Scout moms hit the panic button and search-engined their way to Baxter the Magnificient's show-booking website.

Yeah, they were that desperate.

As the Bunkmobile rumbled onto the gravelly parking lot, we saw girls screaming, moms crying, people hiding under cars. Maybe they'd seen reviews of Baxter's show.

I hopped out of the RV and found a shaken curly-haired Cookie Scout with tears streaking down her freckled face as she sprayed herself with Bug-Be-Gone.

"What's wrong?" I asked. "Out of S'mores?"

"Monsters!" She said stretching the rubber bands in her braces to the breaking point. "BIG HAIRY MONSTERS!!!"

"Monsters?" Baxter poked his head outside the RV window.

I don't guess I have to tell you, but Baxter doesn't believe in monsters, ghosts, ghouls, goblins, aliens, wizards or (apparently) deodorant. But that's another story.

"There's no need to cry, Madame." Baxter skipped off the camper and approached the curly-headed tear hydrant. "Monsters are pretend."

She grabbed the orange and purple hanky from his lapel and pulled it. And pulled it. And pulled it. And pulled it.

"Stop!" Baxter grabbed it as she was about to blow her nose. "That's a magic prop. I don't want you to snot it all up."

"Magic?" She frowned. "Last year we had the Olympic basketball team, and now we get magic? Cookie sales must be lamer than I thought!"

Baxter yanked the endless handkerchief from her hand and tucked it back in his pocket. "Tell me about this so-called monster."

"It showed up in our camp an hour ago. Terrorized some kids. I think it ate my dirty underwear. Well, they may have just gotten mixed up in the laundry bag. But what if they didn't?" Her voice took on a husky whisper. "*What if they didn't*?"

VROOOOOOM! A mini-van with a van full of screaming scouts tore past us. We stepped aside as it roared past. A tent half-hanging off its roof.

A tall, thin woman with dark rimmed glasses and an adult-sized Cookie Scout uniform approached. The nametag on her shirt labeled her as Miss Dumphies.

"Oh, the magician," she said. She scanned the surrounding woods."We're closing down the campsite. I'm afraid there will be no show today."

"Lucky you," I chuckled.

Baxter shot me a look. I smirked. The inner me high-fived myself.

"We must evacuate," Miss Dumphies said. "There's been a Sasquatch sighting!"

"Sasquatch?" Baxter raised his eyebrows. "You saw a Sasquatch?"

"I saw the photo," she said.

"Can I see that photo?" Baxter asked.

"And here we go again," I said, and sat on a nearby log to check my hair for ticks.

Miss Dumphies glared at Baxter. "If you must," she said, "We can go visit Emmy Millhouse. She took this snapshot down by the river and posted it on her Insta-Message site."

Miss Dumphies turned and started walking off. I think we were supposed to follow her.

"But I should warn you," she called back. "She's a fifth-level Cookie Scout. Her word is unimpeachable!"

I sighed. "Oh, he'll peach her, don't worry."

Miss Dumphies led us to a lime green tent that stood just at the edge of the camp. Emmy came out of it and showed Baxter her phone with the selfie on it.

"Photobombed by Bigfoot," I said, and I have to admit, I was a little jealous. She was going to get a million views with that.

Baxter rubbed his chin. "Must be a man in a suit."

I looked around. There were no men here, except for Uncle Danny snoozing in the Bunkmobile. Just moms and girls, none of them big enough to fill out a ferocious Bigfoot suit and none weird enough to own one. "The picture looks real pretty real, Baxter. Besides, what's so hard to believe about Bigfoot? Lots of people have seen him."

"Bigfoot? Ha! A huge monster living in the woods and nobody can take a picture or find any evidence or old monster bones?"

"Well, I took a picture," Emmy Millhouse reminded him. "And you might want to see this!" She took a few steps closer to where the water should have been and pointed to the ground. "Here's more evidence."

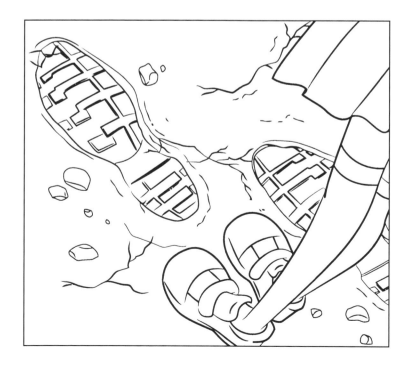

Miss Dumphies smirked. "So whaddya say now, Mr. Science?"

Baxter stared down at them and grinned. "I say the show starts in ten minutes."

"What?!" Dumphies waved her clipboard at the woods. "You can't do magic with a monster on the prowl."

"No. But there is no monster...and I can prove it. All you have to do is look at the pictures."

Again with the pictures? Okay, dear readers, I'm gonna go review the evidence and grab some S'mores.

Time for you to do the same, then read on for Baxter's big reveal.

Okay. Did you figure it out? I gotta admit, I didn't.

But who cares? I had S'mores!!!.

Baxter pointed to the large monster print. "First off, this footprint has shoe-tread."

"Well...maybe there's a Big Foot Locker somewhere around here," I said through a mouthful of marshmallow. I thought it was pretty funny, but no one laughed.

"I can guarantee you this footprint was not made today," Baxter said. "The river has run dry. There hasn't been rain in days. This footprint was made in mud. It wasn't made this summer."

Miss Dumphies folded her arms. "But look at its size! Surely, that was made by a monster."

Baxter knelt beside it. "Or a basketball player. A seven footer even. I'd estimate a size nineteen."

"The Olympic basketball guys from last summer," I remembered. "Okay, but what about the selfie? That monster is way too hairy for a basketball player. He'd look gross in shorts and a tank-top."

"Easily explained," Baxter said. "Emmy faked the picture."

Miss Dumphies gasped. "How dare you?" she said. "She's a fifth-level!"

But Emmy didn't seem so surprised.

Baxter pointed at the sash she wore, the same one that was in the selfie. "Emmy has a Computer Graphic Design merit badge."

"She'd know how to 'composite' a picture," Baxter said.

"Comp-a-what now?" Miss Dumphies asked.

"You can take a picture of someone in front of a green screen, and using a computer you can put whatever you want in the background," I told her. "The Eiffel tower, the Whitehouse..."

"The Bigfoot from the made for cable SQUATCHNADO MOVIE," Baxter put in, and Emmy closed her eyes.

Busted!

"The kids watched that wretched movie last night on their phones." Miss Dumphies said. "But where would a Cookie Scout get a green screen in the middle of the woods?"

I pointed to Emmy's still erected tent. Lime green. "That should do it," I told her.

Miss Dumphies looked at Emmy. Emmy bit her lip.

"While all that 'may' be possible," Miss Dumphies allowed, "as Scout Leader I have to believe in my girls. There's no way you can actually one-hundred percent prove this is a fake."

"There is one thing," Baxter said. "Look at the picture again. There's one thing in the picture that proves this selfie is a fake."

"Look behind her. You can see the rapids. But there isn't a drop of water in this entire area. That's why I was called in to perform — the drought has dried up every creek and river within miles of here. Those rapids are dry. This picture is fake!"

"We'll need a moment," Miss Dumphies said, and pulled Emmy away by her ear.

I watched them go. "I have a feeling she's not going to be fifth-level much longer."

"What puzzles me," Baxter said, "is why would she do this?"

"She was bored," I told him. "Haven't you ever been bored?"

Baxter pulled out a big coin and made it tumble across his knuckles, one way, then the other, defying gravity. I'd seen him do it a hundred times, but still it seemed like magic.

"No," he said.

CHAPTER TWELVE
HOUSTON, TX

"They say you're a skeptic," the Man in the Tin Foil Hat said to Baxter.

Of the many reasons to wear tin foil on your head, fashion is not one. See for yourself.

Baxter admitted to being the skeptic guy. If by "admitted" you mean he said, "you better believe it!"

The Man in the Tin-Foil Hat gave him a superior smile. "Do your worst," he invited. "No way you can change my mind!"

We were busy putting away the props after a show at a car lot. Outdoor shows are the worst, partly because it gets hot in the Lovely Assistant outfit, even with my alterations, but also because there are never curtains on the stage, so people can watch us pack things away.

It makes me feel exposed, like I'm changing clothes in the school lunchroom. But with Baxter, there's another reaction. He gets paranoid about it. He thinks someone might be watching to see how he does his tricks.

Me, I think you'd have to be crazy to watch the show in the first place.

Which brings us back to the Tin-Foil Hat guy.

"I don't want to change anyone's mind," Baxter told him. "I want you to change my mind."

"Is that right?" Mr. Tin-Foil said. "Well, then, what about your famous wager?"

Hmm, again with the wager business? I busied myself with pretending to pack a crate and eavesdropped. I needed to find out more about this wager stuff. What are the rules?

Baxter produced his own hat (not tin foil), reached inside, and pulled up the wad of cash he somehow kept hidden in there. I still don't know how it's hidden, and I've looked. Just for the record, he doesn't keep the piggy-bank in there with it.

Mr. Tin-Foil pulled out a five-dollar bill and said, "Prove to me UFOs don't exist!"

99

Baxter shook his head, and put his wad back in his hat. "I won't do that," he said.

Ooh, I thought, *this should be good!* Baxter never turns down a chance to poke a hole in someone's oddball fantasy.

"Ha!" Tin Foil exclaimed. "Have I stumped the Magnificent Baxter?"

"Hardly," Baxter replied. "I refuse the wager upon three separate points."

Three? If there's anything Baxter likes more than making people look like chumps, it's making lists of ways to make people look like chumps.

"First point," Baxter started, "I refuse because you stated up front that you would never change your mind. Assuming you are coming from a position of already believing in UFOs, then I'd be a fool to take the bet."

Mr. Tin-Foil nodded. "That's a good point."

Baxter wasn't done. "Second, in most cases, it is impossible to prove a negative. Had you come to me asking to disprove a particular UFO sighting, I might've been interested. But how am I to prove something that is not present could never be present? Preposterous!"

I slapped my crate closed and sat on it. This eavesdropping wasn't anywhere near as informative as I was hoping it would be.

"And finally," Baxter concluded, "I refuse because UFOs are real."

I nearly swallowed my tongue. When I got over my coughing fit, I could see that Mr. Tin-Foil was almost as shocked as I was.

"You mean," he said to Baxter, "that you believe there are extraterrestrial visitors to our planet? There's somebody out there?"

"I mean nothing of the sort," he said. "The UFO is an accepted military acronym for an Unidentified Flying Object, and there can be no doubt that certain objects in the sky may go unidentified."

He pointed up at some dot in the sky, barely large enough to see. "For instance, I cannot tell without a doubt what that is. I presume it's an airplane, but perhaps it's a weather balloon, or even a space station or satellite catching a reflection in the sunshine."

He turned back to Tin-Foil. "I have no reason to assume it — whatever it may be — carries little green men."

That was enough to inspire Mr. Tin-Foil to rant about how no one talked about little green men anymore, and that's about when I stopped listening.

"This isn't teaching me anything about the wager," I said to myself, and I must've said it out loud, because there was a voice behind me —

"The Magician's Wager is an old tradition."

It was the Mustache guy again. I hadn't seen him since my first show.

"I like your new look," he said.

I did a little twirl, showing him the whole outfit. "I designed it myself," I said, then remembered. "Wait, what do you know about this wager-thingie?"

"Houdini had one," he told me. "You know who Houdini is?"

"I have to live with Baxter," I said. "Of course I know who he is."

"All the great magicians have an obligation to expose charlatans," he started, but I cut him off.

"I got the charlatan talk, too," I told him. "What's this got to do with a wager?"

"A magician also has to be sure that he is not himself a charlatan," the Mustache went on. "The Wager is there to keep him honest."

"I don't follow," I said. "How does a bet keep him honest? All of these wager people have been trying to fool Baxter."

The Mustache rustled a bit as the man behind it nodded. "That's going to be the case, most of the time. But it's the other times that matter. The Wager is there for the times when he can't debunk. You heard him yourself..."

"I did?" *What did I hear him say?* I wondered.

And then, as if he was reading my mind, the Mustache said, "He doesn't want to change anyone's mind...he wants someone to change *his mind.*"

"You think so?" I asked. "But Baxter thinks he knows everything!"

"The boy is practical," the Mustache said. "He knows what he does not know. You heard him about UFOs?"

"Well, sure, but he had a good reason for that," I said.

"Yes," the Mustache said. "He did. He answered using the information at his disposal. There are things he can't know yet, not until he has access to files at a high level of clearance."

"Clearance?" I looked closer at the Mustache. "I thought you were with the Magician's Palace. Are you some sort of secret agent?"

A soft chuckle came from under his lip-shrub. "The secrets I know," he said, "no agent could ever learn."

"But you think Baxter will?" I asked.

The Mustache said, "He might, if he can keep his mind open to things he does not yet know. You keep him guessing. Keep it up, and maybe it'll be both of you who learn the secrets."

Could that be true? The Baxter I thought I knew was stubborn and in no way interested in anything that might be even slightly outside the realm of reality. Foofaraw, he'd say. Poppycock! Could he really be interested in something that would change the way he sees the world?

I turned to ask the Mustache, but he wasn't there. Just an empty spot where he once was, like a negative that could never be proved.

He must be a secret agent for the Magician's Palace. That vanish was impressive.

·

CHAPTER THIRTEEN
GERTIE'S, WEST TEXAS

The one good thing about traveling the U.S. by Bunkmobile was the milkshake and pancake breakfasts. That morning, I mixed in an apple, but it wasn't for health reasons.

"Hey, Hou-dummy," I said to Baxter across the table. I slurped down a straw full of Peanut Butter and Jelly Ice Cream as I waited for his response.

Baxter didn't seem to hear me. He'd come back to the table after trying to call his parents, but they hadn't answered. They hadn't answered last night, either. I figured they were out getting pictures on the Hollywood Walk of Fame, or comparing their feet to the ones in the cement at the Chinese Theater, but it seemed to worry Baxter.

"Hey," I said again, this time tossing a wadded-up napkin at him. "I want to take the challenge."

He began to choke. Maybe I shouldn't have sprung this on him when he had a mouth full of bran muffin. "My challenge?" He forced through it. "*The* challenge?"

"How much is it? Five dollars?" I raised a folded five-dollar bill from my pocket.

Baxter shook his head. "I won't take your money."

"Of course you won't." I stirred my drink. "I'm going to take your money."

"That's not what I mean," he said. "You're my assistant, you're my cousin. You can't take the challenge."

"I thought your wager was for science. There's no 'cousins' in science." I reconsidered. "Okay, I mean sure, maybe there's cousin-ology or some weird cousin science-ey thing. But not here."

Baxter crossed his arms. "I won't do it."

I slurped the last remnants of my milkshake. "I don't think this challenge of yours is about science at all. I think you're just doing it so you can prove everyone wrong and show them how smart you are."

"That is untrue," Baxter said. "The challenge is a magical tradition! Houdini did it! The Amazing Randi too!"

"Sounds like a smarty-pants tradition," I said.

"Or a truth-ey-pants tradition!" Baxter shouted a little too loud, drawing some attention from other pancake eaters and coffee drinkers. Baxter took a deep breath and shifted back to his inside-voice. "Most people these days believe anything they see or read."

"That's totally not true," I said.

"Guys, check this out!" Uncle Danny lumbered back from the bathroom, reading off his phone. "The Loch Ness monster is secretly living in an aquarium outside of Jersey run by space-aliens. That's why we can't find him. Makes sense, right?"

Baxter turned up his hands in a 'see what I mean?' gesture.

I snatched the phone away from Uncle Danny before he read the related 'Bigfoot gets waxed' story.

"This is different." I held up the phone."Feast your eyes on —

cellphone hypnosis."

Baxter put down his utensils. "You must be joking."

"Oh, it's serious business. I read about it on an internet pop-up ad."

Uncle Danny went for his phone, but I held it out of reach.

"Basically, it allows me to perform feats of strength otherwise thought to be impossible." I stole one of Baxter's celery sticks and tried to snap it in half. It wouldn't break. Celery is stronger than it looks.

"Hypnosis can't make someone perform acts their body isn't capable of." Baxter snatched his celery back and crunched into it.

"So you'll take the bet?" I raised a brow, sensing his curiosity.

Baxter crunched, curiously. Crunch-crunch-crunch.

"What's the amazing feat? Are you going to lift a car?" Uncle Danny leaned forward. "Ooh, or rip a telephone book in half? Do they still have telephone books?"

I raised the apple in front of my face and plucked the straw from my milkshake glass."I will pierce this apple with a straw." I said with my theater voice, drawing a few looks from the nearby breakfasters.

Baxter laughed. "That's impossible."

"Without self-hypnosis...perhaps...but with it, I'm an apple-piercing mean mamma-jamma."

Uncle Danny picked up his own apple and straw, aimed it, then with a primal 'Hi-ya' began stabbing it like a crazed psycho in some old movie. His straw bent and twisted and didn't make even the slightest dent.

"Baxter's right. It's impossible," Uncle Danny said.

My fingers slid the money across the table. "Five dollars says I can."

"Challenge accepted." Baxter slapped a saltshaker on top of the bill. "But this is only for scientific purposes." He picked up the unopened straw the waitress had placed beside his milk carton and handed it to me. "We'll use my straw, of course."

"Of course." I jammed the straw onto the table so the paper scrunched down, then blew the paper right into his face.

I raised the phone to my face and clicked a few buttons. An hourglass spun dizzyingly on the display. I locked my unblinking eyes on it.

Baxter snuck a peek. "That's the download symbol."

"To the untrained eye, perhaps. But by staring at it for just long enough…" My jaw went slack and my body stiffened. "Must kill apple. Must kill apple."

A crowd began to gather, most of them drinking with broken straws.

I turned toward the table like a robot and grabbed the straw.

Everyone backed up, not wanting to be straw-stabbed by a mind-controlled maniac.

"Braaaaaains." I aimed the straw at the apple, reared back, and attacked!

"It must be a trick!" Baxter grabbed the apple. "It's obviously a fake apple. You've hollowed it out." He squeezed the fruit with both hands but it didn't bend, budge or break.

He peered through the straw and glared right at me. "It's... impossible."

"Pay up, cuz," I said going to town on my pancake stack. "Your piggy-bank is now mine!"

CHAPTER FOURTEEN
THE I-10, STILL IN TEXAS!

I decided my bacon bank needed a tour of the Bunkmobile — in the kitchen where Baxter was practicing his cups and balls routine.

Serious gloating would ensue.

Baxter was on his cell phone, pacing and whispering.

"Mom, please call me back," he whispered. "I tried calling Dad too. I'm worried. Please call me back the moment you get this." He paused and I think he wiped some tears from his eyes. "I miss you."

He was using his cell phone. Things must be bad.

"Berni?" he called.

I forced a smile and hid the bacon bank behind me. "Oh... hey cuz...was just looking for my...headphones."

He cocked a brow. "You're wearing your headphones."

"Oh," I said. "Duh. That's why that music is blaring in my ears. Thought I was hearing voices."

"Did you hear what I was talking about?" He squinted as if he was trying to read my mind.

"No. How could I hear if I was listening to the earphones I was looking for?" I nervously giggled.

He stepped closer, zeroing in on the arm I was holding behind my back. "Is that my piggy-bank?"

"Oh, yeah, that." Suddenly, rubbing it in his sad face didn't seem as fun. "I have a confession to make." I sat at the table and waved for Baxter to sit across from me. "I don't really have a phone hypnosis app."

He scratched his head. "But how did you do the thing with the straw?"

"It's a trick. A science-ey trick. You'll like it, being a man of science and all."

Baxter sat down across from me.

I flipped to a bookmarked video on my phone. "The good news is the video of you being fooled went viral."

He frowned.

"Yeah. Maybe that's not good news. But what do one million two hundred thousand viewers know anyway?" I showed him the screen. The video was titled: "DEBUNKER BUNKED." One of the diner patrons had recorded it on their phone and posted it. I fast-forwarded to the part where Uncle Danny and the other diners were trying to stab the apple.

Http://www.cluetube.com/watch/Baxter-got-owned

≡ Clue Tube   Search

▷   ▷| ◁)))   0:36 / 1:40   ⚙   [ ]

DEBUNKER BUNKED!!   1,200,451 views

"Here's the clue." I said. "As you can see, this isn't working."
Beside it, I brought up a second picture, of me stabbing the
apple with much success. "Can you see the difference between
the two pictures?"

Baxter's eyes grew wide. "It's your thumb. Your thumb is covering the end of the straw."

"Ding. Ding. Ding. Give that magician a prize!" I said. "I learned about it in science camp. It's all about the airflow. Even though air seems like nothing, it really is something."

Baxter scratched his head. "You went to science camp?"

"You bet I did. I built a rocket. Powered a hair dryer from a potato. And accidentally set fire to the chemistry lab. But we don't talk about that part. For legal reasons." I chuckled. "Lawyers."

Baxter groaned and slid away from me on his seat.

"Anyhoo," I waved a hand through the air. "Gases like air, even though they are not visible to our eyes, are made up of molecules just like solid objects."

He nodded. "Fascinating."

I grabbed the magic wand from his breast pocket and pretended it was a straw to demonstrate. "When you try to push the straw into the apple the air gets squished closer together. If your thumb is not over the opposite end of the straw the air just spills out the back."

I covered the back of the wand with my thumb. "However, if your thumb IS blocking the opposite end of the straw, the air is trapped. The straw seems empty, but it isn't. It's full of air."

"That's cool. That's like a trick any kid could do any time." Baxter marveled at the wand.

"It works with potatoes too." I said. "And since you figured me out." I slid the bacon bank to his side of the table. "This is yours."

He stared at it dumbly.

"I gave it a bit of a makeover," I said. "Hope you don't mind."

Baxter beamed. "I like the glasses. The glitter might be a bit much."

"Don't touch the glitter. Took me three hours."

"Okay." He looked me in the eyes. "You could've kept the money. And the bank?""

"We're a team," I smiled.

He nodded. "Thanks."

"No sweat." I yawned. "Time for me to strap into my bunk.

I'll see you in the a.m." I slid away from the table and headed off to bed.

"Hey, Berni."

I stopped. "Yeah?"

"What if I teach you a trick?"

I turned.

"One you could perform at the Magician's Palace? Whaddya think?"

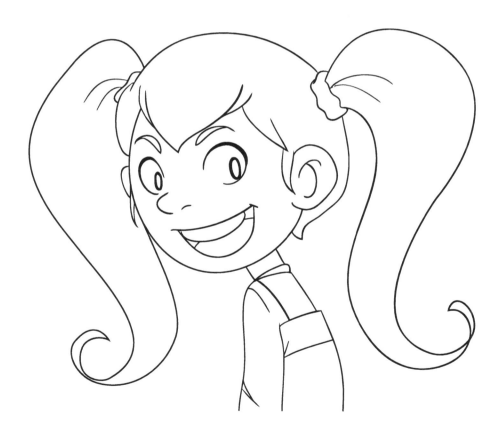

CHAPTER FIFTEEN
EL PASO, TX (FINALLY THE END OF TEXAS!)

We waited behind the stage as an old man stacked red cups into a pyramid in rhythm to a pop song. We were hired to be the headliner for the El Paso Senior Center's annual Fourth of July show, but I wasn't sure we could top this act. The old ladies in the front row were screaming like he was the lead lip-syncher in a boy band.

"So, how about you teach me that magic trick?" I asked Baxter, who was busy adjusting his bow tie.

"Here? Now?" Baxter tugged at his tie. He was only making it worse. "I'm kind of in the middle of something."

I gave the bow tie a quick yank, straightening it for him. "Don't touch it. Or nod." He wanted to, but instead just kind of nodded with his eyes.

"Now," I said, "teach me some Hocus Pocus stuff."

"Okay." Baxter pulled out his sterling silver half-dollar.

He could make it dance between his knuckles, and he loved it like a normal boy might love ice cream, or a puppy.

"This is for you," he said.

My eyes went wide. "Really? For me?"

"I expect you to practice with it every spare minute," he told me. "Every beginning magician needs to learn a good coin trick."

"Like what?" I asked. "Am I supposed to pull it out from behind your ear?"

"I'll teach you a simple vanish," he said. "Watch closely."

Baxter pinched the silver half-dollar between the thumb and index finger of his left hand, and held it in front of me.

He then showed me his right hand. Empty. "You reach for it with this hand. And..."

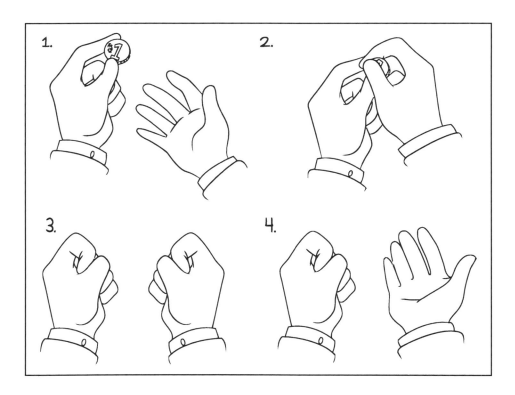

"Not bad," I said. "Where'd it go?"

He opened his left hand, and even though I saw him take it with his right, there it was.

"Misdirection," he said. "It's the basis of all magic."

I nodded. "So, you pretend to take the coin, but it stays in your original hand the whole time."

"Oldest trick in the book," he said.

I gave it a try, but it was clumsy. I dropped it. Clunk! the coin rolled on the floor. I chased it and picked it up.

Baxter looked concerned, like he wasn't entirely sure he should be trusting his favorite coin to me.

"I'll get it," I assured him.

"Takes a lot of practice," he said. "And it's only real if you believe it. That's where the artistry comes in. Do it in front of a mirror until you believe it."

I nodded, gazing at the coin.

Baxter smiled. "You can do it," he told me.

They called our names and we marched out to the thundering applause of three napping senior citizens.

CHAPTER SIXTEEN
AFTER THE SHOW

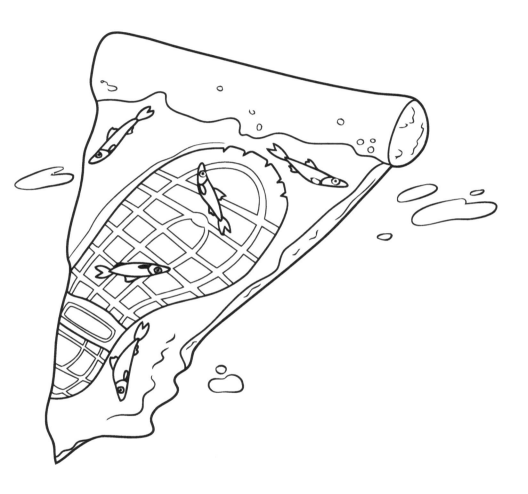

"We've been robbed!" Uncle Danny shouted as he entered the Bunkmobile.

"How can you tell?" I asked. "This is how it always looks."

Uncle Danny wasn't big on the whole "cleaning" thing. He pointed to the floor. A leftover pizza had a footprint in it. "Someone stepped in my extra anchovies."

"No loss there," I said, stifling a gag. I was more of a pepperoni and extra cheese girl.

Baxter rushed to Uncle Danny's bedroom, where he kept all his magic supplies.

"Baxter! Wait, it might not be safe!" Uncle Danny hurried after him.

So did I. I didn't want to be alone with anybody crazy enough to rob this trash heap.

Baxter's props and magic equipment had been rummaged through. Baxter was a bit of a neat freak. Everything had its own drawer and nook and cranny. To see everything spilled out, it was obvious, we'd been robbed!!

Uncle Danny said, "I wonder what they were after?"

I grabbed the piggy bank. It sat unscathed. "Obviously not money."

"Secrets." Baxter shoved scattered papers into a folder. The papers were blueprints for new tricks. They looked like mere doodles, but to Baxter they were everything. "Someone's been going through my new trick file! This is a travesty! We need to call the —"

"Police?" A voice came from behind us.

It was The Mustache.

He weaved through the clutter and into the room. He pulled the long whiskers away from his chest to reveal a shiny badge.

"So, at last you come out of the shadows," Baxter said. "He's been following us since Florida."

"Phew!" I let out a breath. "You saw him too? Thank goodness! I was worried I was imagining him." I looked at the Mustache. Officer Mustache, I guess. "So you're a cop?"

"A detective, actually. Did someone report a robbery?" he said. At least, I think it was him. Hard to tell since his lips were buried beneath a forest of whiskers. He'd make a killing as a ventriloquist.

"We were about to," Uncle Danny said.

"I'm good at my job." The Mustache flipped open one of those little note pads cops are always jotting things down in on TV. He clicked his pen three times and twirled it around in his fingers like a baton. A neat trick. "Now, what's missing?"

Uncle Danny shrugged. "Nothing, I guess."

"Apparently, they read my cousin's diaries or something," I said.

"Trade secrets!" Baxter raged. "Intellectual property!"

"Hmm." Mustache scribbled a bit in the book. "Do you have any idea who could have done this?"

"Besides you?" Baxter asked.

The Mustache chose not to write that in his little pad. "Have you seen any mysterious characters around?"

"Again, you," Baxter said.

"Ridiculous," he responded. "Why would you be suspicious of an officer of the law?"

"Well, the pizza on your shoe, for starters." Baxter pointed.

Mustache plucked it off and sniffed it. "I don't know how it got there. I must've stepped on it on the way in."

"When you were breaking-and-entering, you mean?" I said.

Baxter narrowed his eyes at the Mustache. "I think it's time you explained why you've been following us."

"And why you've been stepping on our pizza," Uncle Danny said.

Mustache tucked his notes away and leveled us with a steely gaze from just above his whiskers. "I'm looking for the boy's parents. They've gone missing."

Baxter gritted his teeth.

"Missing? That's not true," Uncle Danny said. "They're performing at the Magic Palace. We're meeting them there in a week."

"They were performing there until last night," Mustache said. "They were the only ones backstage when something went missing — the Crystal Ball of Nostradamus."

"The Crystal Ball donated to the Palace's magic museum?" Baxter asked.

"Isn't that worth like a gazillion dollars?" I said. "Jackson Plateau bought it in an auction two years ago."

"And donated it to the museum," Mustache confirmed. "It's been kept in a special vault ever since, and only brought out in special occasions. Last night, it was stolen by the Amazing Bunkhouses."

"You're lying!" Baxter shouted. "My parents would never steal anything."

"When was the last time you saw them?" Mustache cocked his whiskers.

"Two weeks ago," Uncle Danny said. "They dropped Baxter off at the carnival, then went to the airport."

"Two weeks," Mustache noted on his pad. "And they were headed to the Magician's Palace?"

"They were invited guests," Baxter said.

Mustache flipped his pad closed with a dramatic flourish. He should be on TV. "Have you talked to them? Since they fled the Palace?"

"Now wait just a minute," Uncle Danny said. "Baxter talks to them every night on the phone. Don't you Baxter?"

All eyes turned to Baxter. He looked like he might cry. And as much as I'd wanted to torment him just days before, we'd become a team. I had to get his back.

"Where's your proof?" I growled. "We're magicians. We know how easy it is to deceive. If you want our help, we need proof."

"I have witnesses," Mustache declared. "The Crystal Ball

was taken out and shown to a gathering of magicians just before the show. It was placed back into the large vault at the same time by the president of the Palace. No one was backstage but a security guard, and cameras show the vault was never opened. Then we got an anonymous tip."

"A tip?" I asked.

"A tip," Mustache confirmed. "That the Bunkhouses took it. During their water tank escape. While we thought they were in the tank they were actually in the vault. We went to the vault and verified it hadn't been opened. But when we opened it, the Crystal Ball was gone."

Mustache produced a photo marked "EVIDENCE."

"See the water?" Mustache pointed. "There's your evidence. They came to it straight from the water tank!"

I glared at him. "But you said the vault was never opened!"

"It wasn't," Mustache said. "Which means," and he gave a long, dramatic pause here, "someone walked through the walls!"

The walking-through-walls trick was The Amazing Bunkhouses closer. Everyone knew it.

"That's just a trick. It can only be done on stage," Baxter explained.

Mustache pulled out his notebook again. "A trick? Then tell me...how is it done?"

Baxter crossed his arms. "I can't tell you. It's against the magician's code."

The Mustache got right in Baxter's face. "Well, if you don't tell me, your parents are going to end up IN PRISON!"

"That's enough, fuzzy-face," Uncle Danny said, stepping between him and Baxter. "You gonna slap the cuffs on a twelve-year-old?"

I put my arm around Baxter's shoulders and pulled him aside. "Look, I know there's a magician's code and all, but maybe you should just tell him. Stealing is a serious matter. If you can clear your parents' name, maybe you should just do it."

Baxter shook his head. "I might, if I could. But I have no idea how it's done. It's a mystery. No magician has ever figured out how it's done. Not even me."

"Then how do you know it's a trick?" the Mustache said. "Maybe they can really do it!"

"I know it's a trick," Baxter snapped, "Because my parents are magicians, not ghosts!"

"Are you so sure about that?" the Mustache taunted. "I've watched you. You're the best debunker around. Ever wonder why you can't debunk them?"

Baxter had nothing to say to that.

"I'll see myself out," The Mustache said, all dramatic again, like someone was going to guide him the ten feet to the door. This guy put on a better show than Baxter.

"Go buy yourself a razor, Fur-lock Holmes," Uncle Danny called after him, then muttered to us, "Some detective... phooey!"

"What now?" I asked Baxter.

"Now," Baxter said, his face no longer afraid, but instead angry. "Now, we go straight to the Magician's Palace! No stops for pancakes!"

CHAPTER SEVENTEEN
THE AMAZING BUNKHOUSES!

Guess it's time we talked about Baxter's parents.

Uncle Manny and Aunt Winnie. They're cool. They never forget my birthday, always sending a card that looks empty at first, then some money or a gift card appears in it — you get that kind of thing when you have magicians in the family.

"The Amazing Bunkhouses" is the name they use when they're on-stage, and they're kind of famous. Magician-famous, you understand, not movie-star-famous. They never got a TV special or anything.

But still, kind of famous.

The big closer to their show is the Walking Through The Wall trick.

As they performed, a bricklayer built a wall of bricks right on the stage in full view of the audience.

Baxter's' parents took positions on opposite sides of the wall then ran full speed directly at it. I wanted to close my eyes. I'd seen enough face-smash videos to know how this ended.

But they never smashed. Not a brick out of place, and still they went right through without so much as an "ouch."

People have been trying to figure it out for years, but no one knows how it's done. Including, it seems, their son.

But it's just a trick, right? No one can really walk through walls.

Right?

CHAPTER EIGHTEEN
NON-STOP!

Uncle Danny had driven for twelve straight hours. We were still a day away, even driving without stops (except for gas and bean burritos). Which was okay since I needed to work on my big magic trick.

Baxter paced inside the Bunkmobile like a caged tiger (well, rabbit), even when Uncle Danny made a stop to gas up (gasoline this time, not chili).

He was using his cell phone again, trying to connect to his parents. Obsessively.

"Where could they be?" he asked. "They must be in trouble."

"It's okay," I said. "You're the great Baxter Bunkhouse. You'll figure it out."

If you want the honest truth, I wasn't so sure.

He wasn't himself.

He'd always been annoying, and a little stinky, and had never been exactly my cup of tea. But if there's one thing he always had, it was confidence.

He looked scared.

Baxter was used to his parents being a phone call away. Now that they had been accused of stealing, they seemed to have gone into hiding.

It made sense. Jail stinks. And Detective Mustache really wanted to put them there. And since they didn't do it (and no, there's no chance they did it), what else could they do except stay out of the way until the crime was solved?

Whatever the case, Baxter was rattled.

And I needed to do something about it.

CHAPTER NINETEEN
THE BLACK HOLE OF ARIZONA!

"There it is," I said to Uncle Danny. "Next exit."

I was up front with him, navigating.

Baxter poked his head in. "Already? How did we get here so soon?"

Uncle Danny grabbed the dashboard GPS. "What? Someone must have reprogrammed the GPS."

That someone would've been me. "Hmmm. Weird. Well, since we're here. We might as well have a look."

I'd found the place by looking online, but I could've just sat up there and watched billboards pass. They were warning us it was coming for fifty miles.

The Black Hole of Arizona — its website told me it was a "Mystic Vortex for All that is Supernatural in the Southwest!" It also told me there was a gift shop. Uncle Danny grabbed the dashboard GPS. "What? Someone must have reprogrammed the GPS."

What it didn't tell me, I was able to fill in for myself.

This place was the number one Charlatan Headquarters on the road to California, and if this couldn't pull Baxter out of his funk, nothing could.

"Why are we stopping?" Baxter asked. "We're on a schedule."

"Uncle Danny's got to get gas, anyway," I told him. "And we're low on burritos."

That part wasn't entirely true — Baxter really hadn't been eating, and I'd had about all the burrito I wanted for the rest of my life — but technically, we hadn't eaten for a few hours and it was time. "Besides, you need to get out."

"I'll wait here," he said. "We need to get moving as quickly as possible."

"No, you're missing the point," I said. "You haven't moved in a day, and you're growing moss." I opened the door. "Walk. Exercise. Get out."

Baxter didn't see my logic, so I shoved him.

In the sunlight, he hissed like a vampire and shielded his eyes.

"See?" I told him. "You've been in there too long."

He wanted to move into the shade of the building, but I held him in place long enough for his eyes to adjust so he could read the sign.

"Hmm," Baxter said.

I led him inside.

A bell over the door gave a little "ping" as we entered, and a woman behind a glass counter looked up from her game of solitaire and pointed. "Candy's over there, sodas there, fireworks are in the back."

Ooh, fireworks!

But Baxter had another focus. "I'm here to see this Black Hole of yours."

The woman raised her eyebrows approvingly, then reached under her counter and pulled up a bright green turban. She put it on, and then put on an accent that sounded like it came straight from a cartoon.

"Velcome," she said. "I am Madame Velda!"

I wondered if that meant her name was "Welda" and the weird accent altered it, or if she was really a Velda. Either way, she probably made the name up.

She shuffled out from behind the counter, and surprised me by stepping down a few steps. She was shorter than we were, even though she was probably about a thousand years older. Or at least forty.

"Follow Madame Velda," she said. "She vill reveal all!"

She turned and walked toward a door in the back.

I looked at Baxter. "Have you seen enough already?" Baxter didn't say anything, and followed Madame Velda. I shrugged and tagged along.

Madame Velda looked back at us, doing a lot of work with her eyebrows and bugging her eyes. "Through this door lies mystery to boggle the imagination!" She lowered her eyebrows and squinted at us. "Are you villing to vitness such vonders?"

It took me a minute to translate that from Silly Accent-ese, but I got it. We both nodded.

Madame Velda pushed through the door into blackness.

A clear plastic box was mounted beside the door, a few dollars and coins inside of it. The printing on the front read "Suggested donation: 50 cents."

All I had was my magic fifty-cent piece, and I wasn't about to put that in there. Baxter stuffed a dollar into the slot on top of the box.

And then ve vent in. Er, I mean, we went in.

Madame Velda was waiting for us beside a case with an open top. "Behold!" she intoned. "The Mummified Remains of General George Armstrong Custer!"

"General Custer died at the Battle of Little Big Horn," Baxter said. "That's in Montana."

"And yet," Madame Velda countered, "here he is! Mystery!"

She shuffled off into the shadows.

"Mystery indeed," Baxter muttered, but we continued the tour.

A light came on a few yards down a roped-off path. "Now," Madame Velda waved her arm at a giant mask on the wall, "gaze in terror upon the Face of the Aztec Giant Tehocoutlan!"

"Wait," I said. "The face? You took the face off a giant?"

"That looks Polynesian in design," Baxter added. "What was that name you said?"

But Madame Velda was already moving on. "Mystery!" came her voice as she again disappeared into the darkness between exhibits.

We crept through the shadows, and the floors got uneven. I felt like I was walking on an incline, then another to the side, and then we got to a rope that crossed the path. Beyond that was more darkness.

A light flashed on, illuminating a room on the other side of the rope. A table leaned sharply to the right. Madame Velda walked to the low end of the table. "And finally, ve reach the True Center of the Vortex, vhere gravity holds no svay!"

She pulled an orange from the folds of her robe and placed it on the low end of the table — and it rolled uphill to the other end!

I clapped my hands in appreciation. The rest of it had been kind of silly, but this was a good trick! "How did you do that?" I asked.

"In the Black Hole," Madame Velda said, "all is possible!"

"We're standing on a slant," Baxter told me. "It's an optical illusion. The ball is really rolling downward, as usual, but from our angle it appears to defy gravity."

The light went off, and another came on over a door in the distance. Baxter and I walked to it and back out into the gift shop.

Amazingly, the short lady was already back behind her glass countertop. "So how was the Black Hole?" she asked, all traces of ridiculous accent gone. "Was it everything you'd hoped?"

I stepped back to give Baxter his space. Plus, I didn't want to be hit by any stray sarcasm.

"It was quite entertaining," Baxter smiled. "Thank you."

And he walked out into the sunlight.

I watched him go, then looked at the tiny woman who used to be Madame Velda. "What was that?" I asked.

She'd gone back to her solitaire. "Another satisfied customer."

I caught up with Baxter as he climbed into the Bunkmobile.

"Baxter," I asked. "What happened? She was a charlatan!

She was presenting this as magic, taking money for it, and you just walked away!"

Baxter nodded. "It was a show. She didn't even demand money, just a 'suggested donation.' And did you see the way she dressed? She might as well have been on a stage," he said. "She was doing it for fun.

"But thank you," he said. "Now I'm ready."

CHAPTER TWENTY
CALIFORNIA, HERE WE COME!

"Hooray," **Baxter and I** cheered. "We're almost there!"

And then everything stopped.

"We'll still get to the Palace by dark," Uncle Danny said from behind the wheel. "If we can find a place to leave the Bunkmobile."

"Why don't we just park it in front of the Magician's Palace?" I asked.

Uncle Danny looked at me. "You've never been to Los Angeles, have you? There's almost no such thing as street parking, and even if there were a spot —" He waved his hand out the windshield at the unmoving traffic. "You think we could find one big enough for the Bunkmobile?"

And so we sat in the back of the Bunkmobile. Waiting.

At one point, Uncle Danny left the front seat and came back to get a grape soda out of the refrigerator.

"Shouldn't you be driving?" I asked.

He popped open the soda and strolled back to the front. "I am," he said.

There was no increase (or decrease) in the car-horn-honking while he was away, so I guess there wasn't any movement out there.

I practiced my coin trick, and Baxter gave me some helpful tips. Which was a little weird. He'd been through some serious changes lately.

After more than an hour, during which our mobile home was somewhat less than mobile, Baxter got up.

"The show starts in two hours!!" He grabbed some equipment and loaded it onto our cart. "We've got to go!"

"What are you doing?" I asked.

"If we're late, we'll never figure out what happened to my parents." He opened the door, and bounced the cart out.

"Hey," Uncle Danny said from the front. "What's that?"

"I got it," I told him, and ran out after Baxter. I heard Uncle Danny calling my name, but Baxter wasn't far. I'd be able to get him back.

I don't know if you've ever walked on a highway during rush hour before, but I don't recommend it. It was unnerving, being around all those cars with their engines running. It was like being in a huge parking lot, but no one could get their doors unlocked.

"Baxter!" I called. He was three cars ahead, and I ran up to him.

"I have to get there," Baxter said.

I nodded. "I know, but you don't even know the way." I lifted my phone and showed him the GPS app. "I do."

CHAPTER TWENTY-ONE
A RELAXING WALK

"This is it." Baxter was out of breath, but it wasn't from the walk. After all, I'd been the one pushing the cart most of the time.

"You sure?" My phone GPS agreed with Baxter that this was, indeed, the location of the Magician's Palace. But I didn't see any castles or magic, just a bunch of tall bushes that went right up to the sidewalk. "It doesn't look like the pictures."

But Baxter's eyes were wide as he looked up at the shrubbery. "The Hedges of Wonder!!"

"Hedges of Wonder?" I rolled my eyes.

"They shield the Palace from onlookers," Baxter said. "Only the elite may enter. Even to gaze upon the Magician's Palace is to be one of a chosen few."

Uh-huh. I looked up the place online. I guess Internet access makes me one of the chosen. I checked my watch. "Ninety minutes to show time. You ready for this?"

Baxter took a deep breath and we rolled the gear toward the gate inside the hedges.

Sorry, the HEDGES OF WONDER!!!

And then we saw it.

"It looks like Barbie hired Malibu King Arthur to be the architect of her Dream House," I said.

Baxter just stood there, wide-eyed and speechless.

"If Dracula and Hello Kitty had a baby," I went on, "this is where it would live."

Baxter didn't crack. His eyes were wet.

"This is like the Holy Land for you, isn't it?" I said. "Santa's Workshop, Willy Wonka's Factory, and Disneyworld, all mixed together into one big peppermint-chocolate-mouse-ears parfait."

His lower lip trembled.

"Baxter?" I touched his arm, shook it a little. "Let's go in."

I searched for the doorbell, but there wasn't one. Instead, there was a thick chain that hung down from far overhead, with a silk-wrapped ball at the end, and lots of gold fringe around it. I tugged on it, and inside a huge Chinese gong sounded.

The door swung open.

Baxter made a little whimpering noise in the back of his throat.

No one was inside the door.

We stood there a moment.

"You think we should go in?" I asked.

Baxter didn't respond.

"I think we should go in." I pushed our prop cart through the doorway.

We stopped a few feet inside and peered into the shadows.

BLAM! The door slammed behind us, leaving us in total darkness. And also scaring a yelp out of Baxter. Okay, me too.

"Hello?" I called out. My voice echoed a bit, but nothing more.

"Hello. I'm Baxter Bunkhouse," my cousin said.

A voice answered back, a familiar voice that said, "Why is this light off? Was no one there to greet you as you arrived?"

Then a light flashed on overhead, re-blinding me just as my eyes were adjusting, but when I opened them –

To which I can only add:

EEEEEEEEEEKKKKK!!!

CHAPTER TWENTY-TWO
THE GRAND TOUR

"I've heard great things." Jackson shook Baxter's hand. "Looking forward to seeing you on the stage."

And then he turned to me and –

Sorry, I might've blacked out for a second there.

— then he turned to me and took my hand (JACKSON PLATEAU WAS HOLDING MY HAND!) and said, "You must be Beatrice, the Lovely Assistant."

Beatrice? "Um, it's Bernice," I muttered, then corrected, "Berni. But no one calls me —"

He was already walking away with Baxter. "Let me show you around the Palace," he told him, leaving me to push the cart.

I followed them through a heavy door and found myself in an auditorium. Rows of seats, not as many as my school auditorium, but more than a few, with maroon velvet cushions and red fuzzy wallpaper with brassy trim and little lamps that stood out from the walls at just the right height to catch you in the forehead if you weren't watching for them. It was all about as tacky as used gum.

"It's all so wonderful!" Baxter said.

He and Jackson Plateau (JACKSON PLATEAU!) were already standing on the stage by the time I caught up with them. "Ah, there you are," Jackson Plateau said thoughtfully when he saw me. "You should come up here, too, Bernadette."

At least he was getting closer. I parked the cart and ran around to the stairs and out onto the stage and, well, maybe "wonderful" wasn't quite the word, but it was darned impressive from up there.

"There's still an hour-and-a-half before showtime," Jackson Plateau said. "Perhaps you'd like to run through your act?"

Jackson snapped his fingers and the lights on the stage went out. A spotlight blazed out of the dark, pointing right at us. We'd been on a few stages in our tour, but nothing like this.

154

"We'll definitely need a rehearsal," Baxter told him. "But maybe we should find the dressing room first? We need to unpack and get organized."

"Of course," Jackson Plateau nodded, and put an arm over Baxter's shoulders, leading him away.

Leaving me alone. On the stage. In the spotlight.

I smiled and did a quick shuffle like the one I had learned in that snooty dance class I got kicked out of, and then the spotlight went out.

And I was left to push the cart alone in the dark. Again.

I found them backstage. There were two doors, with a star on each. We each had our own dressing room!

Baxter thanked Jackson Plateau, and then I heard him say, "If it's not too much trouble, I'd like to see the safe."

"The safe?" Jackson Plateau looked a little surprised, so I jumped in.

"Sure, the place where you keep the really rare items," I said. "Houdini's lucky socks, Merlin's favorite golf clubs. They talk about it in all the magician magazines."

Jackson Plateau looked at me like I was crazy. I doubt there are any magician magazines. I'm not even sure there are magazines anymore.

He nodded and took us past the dressing rooms to a stairwell, and in a few seconds, we were looking at it.

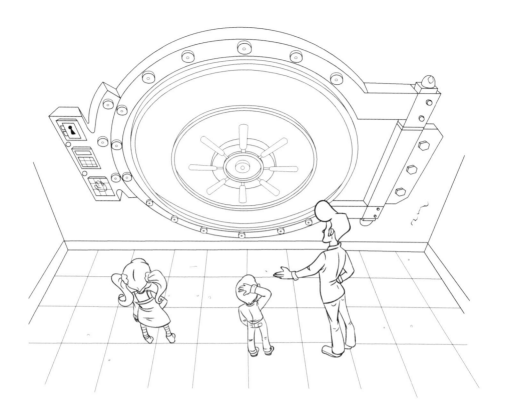

If you could manage to get a freight train through the theater and down those stairs, charging at full speed, I doubt you could even dent this thing. "Wow," I said. "Does that door even open?"

Jackson Plateau put in his key, stuck his hand on the bioreader, and dialed up the combination. "The vault automatically photographs everyone who opens it."

"So there's a record of anyone who enters?" Baxter said hopefully.

"As long as they open the door," Jackson Plateau confirmed. "Of course, if anyone were to, say, walk through a wall without opening the door, there'd be no picture." Jackson Plateau smirked. "But no one could do that, could they?"

156

He gripped the big wheel on the front. It squeaked loudly, as if it hadn't been turned or oiled in years.

The huge door slid open.

I followed Baxter into the vault.

It was bigger than my bedroom, and carpeted red, just like the theater.

Everywhere I looked was a piece of magic history. Houdini's handcuffs, Blackstone's floating light bulb, the first Cups and Balls.

Baxter had eyes for only one of the displays.

The empty pedestal where Nostradamus's Crystal Ball once sat.

"Ah, yes," Jackson Plateau said, noticing Baxter's gaze. "I see you've found the site of our recent loss. Everything in this room is priceless, but that... that was the most priceless."

"I thought you bought it at an auction," I said.

"That's right," Jackson Plateau confirmed.

"Soooo," I said, "you paid for it?"

He nodded.

"Meaning you paid a price?" I asked.

Jackson Plateau looked at me. "What are you getting at, Bonnie?"

"If you paid a price for it, then it couldn't have been priceless," I said. "And it's Berni."

"I think it's time we went to our dressing rooms," Baxter said. "I'd like a few minutes to rehearse on stage before the guests arrive."

"Yes," Jackson Plateau said, ignoring me. I was beginning to not like this guy. "I need to meet the caterers and prepare for tonight's extravaganza."

He left us once we'd made it back to the dressing rooms. "What's with him?" I asked Baxter.

"He's lost a valuable object," Baxter said, "and the Mustache Detective no doubt implicated my parents, and relayed his suspicions that we might know something to reveal them. Under the circumstances, he was quite polite."

158

"I suppose," I said. "But he's starting to bug me. I think I'm going to keep an eye on him."

Baxter shook his head. "Your time may be better served working on your trick," he said. "I'll need you to be a diversion while I search for a secret entry to the safe."

"Diversion? Wait... you mean, while we're on stage?" I suddenly realized what Baxter had in mind. "You're going to leave me up there...*alone*?"

"It's the perfect plan." Baxter cocked a brow. "While everyone is watching you up onstage, I'll be able to investigate."

I pictured myself, up there on the stage, coin in my hand. All those magicians watching only me.

"Is it too late," I asked, "to teach me how to disappear?"

CHAPTER TWENTY-THREE
PRE-SHOW JITTERS

I stood on the stage and stared out at the still empty seats and one thought went through my mind — "Don't vomit."

How many stages had I been on? Dozens. This was the first time I was nervous.

This was also the first time I was doing the trick.

I really should've taken a few practice runs at a birthday party or bar mitzvah. Doing it the first time in front of the collected Greatest Magicians In The World? That was crazy-pants!

The audience lights shined down on the empty seats. The stage lights were off. I wondered if I'd feel better with the spotlight, so I couldn't see out there.

Okay, it was no time for nerves. I had a job to do. I lifted my right hand out in front of me, showing the coin between my fingers. This part I had down pretty good. Baxter had taught me how to hold it so the stage lights bounced off it just right.

I pretended to grab it in my left hand while secretly tucking it into the right. My eyes followed the left hand — misdirection — as I raised it eye level and with a flourish, opened it. Nothing there!

Clank! The coin dropped from its secret location (aka my right hand).

It hit the floor and rolled in a big, wide circle, all the way around me, around and around, it seemed like forever, until it bumped into my foot and clattered to a stop.

This was going to be a disaster.

At least there was no one there to witness. Maybe I still had time to escape.

I looked up the aisle. A door was open. On the other side of it, people pushed carts. I considered crawling into one, letting them roll me out of here. I'd seen that in a prison-escape movie once.

I hurried up the aisle and peeked out the door into the brightly lit lobby.

The carts were loaded with food and drinks, and the people pushing them wore black aprons over white shirts with black bowties. They were setting the food out on a long, polished wood table.

I'd eaten nothing but bean burritos for the last couple of days, and whatever they were putting out smelled delicious.

Just when I'd decided to stroll out casually and announce that I was Mr. Plateau's official food-taster, Jackson Plateau himself entered the scene.

He was talking to a fellow pushing another cart, this one with a tall block on it, draped with black cloth. The cart held a variety of knives and a little silver hammer.

The guy pushing the cart whipped the cloth off to reveal a big piece of ice, carved into the shape of a magician's top hat.

Jackson Plateau picked up some of the utensils off the cart and tapped at the ice a bit, smoothing out some edges.

"You did a great job, Mr. Plateau," the cart guy said.

"Of course I did," Jackson Plateau answered. "I'm me!"

The guy with the cart pulled out a clipboard with paper on it, and handed it to Jackson Plateau with a pen.

Jackson Plateau signed, then clicked the pen three times and twirled it like a baton as he slipped it into his breast pocket.

Wowza! He used to do that on his old TV show, *Bobby Popcorn, NYPD!* Whenever he was interrogating a suspect, he'd write notes in his little spiral notebook and then do a trick with his pen as he put it away in his overalls. How cool!

He must have been doing tricks like that since he was a kid, and now he ran the Magician's Palace. He might be kind of a jerk, but at least he got to do what he'd always wanted to do. You had to admire him for that.

Then I heard the guy with the cart say, "Um, that's my pen."

And Jackson Plateau walked away.

Yeah, he's kind of a jerk.

CHAPTER TWENTY-FOUR
PEEKING THROUGH THE CURTAINS

It was starting to get noisy out there.

Baxter paced the stage, working through all the tricks in his head.

I was pacing, too, trying to remember just how to do the coin trick, and how not to drop the coin in the process.

"Baxter," I whispered, "you don't have any glue, do you? Or duct tape?"

He stopped, looked at me. "What?"

"Never mind." I crept to the curtain, parted it just enough to get an eyeful.

"Stop that!" Baxter hissed, whisking me away. "That's unprofessional!" He shook his head and tsked at me. "When have we ever done something like that? I'm surprised at you!"

"Well," I told him, "this is a different audience than we usually get, isn't it?" I pointed a thumb at the curtain. "You should see some of the freaks out there! I swear I saw one wearing a gasmask!"

"A gasmask?" Baxter's face went pale. "A black gasmask?"

I shrugged. "Do gasmasks come in colors?"

"That's Professor Somnambula!" he shouted.

We both peeked through the curtain.

"Over there," Baxter said. "That's The Mystifying Medici! Ooh, and The Great Gilhooley! And Ankh Amen-Ra! And Stilton the Stupefying!"

"Who are those two in the turbans?" I asked.

Baxter gasped. "Could it be? The Grand Gurus of Gujarat have come out of retirement just to see me?"

My eyes went to the back of the room, and found a familiar face. "Hey, isn't that your favorite plus-sized charlatan?"

"Vinny Vision," Baxter confirmed. "How did he get in here?"

A voice came from behind us. "He had an invitation."

We whipped around to see Jackson Plateau looking at us. "Having a television show grants you certain privileges around here," he said.

"Yeah," I muttered. "I've noticed."

"We've run into Mr. Vision before," Baxter said. "He claims to be a psychic."

Jackson Plateau nodded. "I've seen his work. I'm a fan. I hope to get a private session with him later. Maybe he can tell me what happened to... a certain object we're missing here at the Magician's Palace."

Baxter's eyes barely stayed in his head. "You would employ Vinny Vision? In his, er, "professional" capacity? At the Magician's Palace?"

"Hey, I like to keep an open mind," Jackson Plateau said. "Never know what he might be able to do. We only use ten-percent of our brains, you know."

Even I knew that was a myth, and a silly one at that. We use all of our brains. Well, most of us do, anyway. Can't speak for certain TV actors. Or TV psychics.

"Have a good show, kids," Jackson Plateau said, walking to the front of the stage. "You're on."

Baxter just stared after him as Jackson Plateau pushed past the curtain and out to the audience. I could hear him introducing us.

"Hey?" I shook his arm. "Hey, Baxter, don't check out on me now."

Baxter blinked, and then looked at me. "Did the president of the Magician's Palace just express a belief in the possibility of Vinny Vision's supernatural powers?"

I nodded. "I think. But let's not let it ruin the show."

"I know who took the Crystal Ball of Nostradamus," Baxter said.

And before I could ask him, what he meant by that, the curtain opened, and the show was on.

CHAPTER TWENTY-FIVE
SHOWTIME!

The show was going smoothly.

Baxter did his best tricks, and the audience applauded. Not "this is the most amazing show we've ever seen" applause. Not even "meh, not bad for a kid" applause. But they did clap, and they didn't throw rotten fruit and vegetables, and that was something.

Then we got to the part of the show that made my stomach drop in anticipation.

Baxter wheeled out the booth while I waved my hands at it as if there'd never been a spray-painted black wooden box more beautiful. He spun it, tapping here and there to show that all the sides were solid. There was a curtain across the front, and he pulled it open to show the box was empty, and again tapping to show the sides were solid.

Which they weren't, but no one watching needed to know that.

Next came the part where I was supposed to climb into the booth, and he'd close the curtain and do some alakazam-hooey with his wand and say a magic word, and when he opened it again, I'd be gone.

Only this time, it was Baxter who entered the booth, and it was up to me to do the hocus-pocus and turn myself around. Baxter was going to disappear, and leave me alone on the stage to entertain the audience myself.

He gave me a little wink as he entered, and an encouraging nod. It didn't help.

But I closed the curtain anyway, and started the bit.

Now, magician's code prevents me from telling you exactly how the trick is done, but I feel comfortable letting you know that I've never actually been invisible. As far as I know. By the time the curtain was closed, Baxter was already out of the booth and on his way backstage and down to snoop around the safe.

So when I pulled back the curtain and said — ABRA-KAVOOTIE!!!!

No one was surprised (least of all an audience full of professional magicians who had cut this bit from their acts before Baxter was born) to find it empty.

Still, there was applause. They were at least polite to a fellow magician.

I wondered how they'd greet a semi-pro Lovely Assistant with a cheesy magic trick a child could do.

"Ahem," I said.

Not my best start. I tried again.

"Ladies and gentlemen, lords and lordesses, cats and dogs, before me sit the greatest magicians, mystics and seers from around the world!" That was better. Butter them up.

"Let me introduce myself — I am known as..." and then I stopped.

What was I known as? Just "Berni" seemed a little too ordinary for this crowd, and there was no way I was announcing myself as "The Great Bernice" or "Berndini." "Magnificent" was taken. I feared "Amazing" might be promising more than I could deliver. "Astounding?" "Mind-Boggling?" "Odd?" No, definitely not "Odd."

Well, I'd better come up with a good one, and quick, because if I stayed frozen any longer, Jackson Plateau was going to come out and carve me like one of his ice sculptures.

"Denizens of this planet call me," I went on, "Bunkhouse the... Beginner!"

A soft chuckle trickled through the audience. I might have pushed their politeness as far as it would go.

But there was no stopping now. If I did, someone was sure to wonder where Baxter was, and that wouldn't end well.

"Behold!" I shouted, just like my cousin taught me, and produced the coin in my right hand.

"I now present to you," I intoned in my best magician voice, "the Magic Coin of..." I looked at it to see if it had any name. Nope. "Some Old Guy! Probably a president!"

More laughs, and these weren't so quiet.

My face felt hot. I swallowed and remembered why I was doing this. *Baxter in the basement,* I reminded myself, *Baxter in the basement.*

Every eye in the place was glued to my right hand. They knew the trick. They'd done it themselves. Misdirection. You fake-grab with the left hand but keep the coin in the right.

And so, in front of all those magic eyes in all those magic heads, I did the trick, they'd seen more than any other.

I held the coin out with my right, grabbed the coin with my left, raised the left hand in the air.

Smiled.

And opened.

The coin was in it.

Uh-oh. Instead of faking it, I'd actually grabbed it. Just the way it looked like I had. Just exactly the opposite of what I was supposed to do. I'd been so nervous about getting the moves right, about putting on a good magic show, that I'd forgotten to make the switch.

There was a collective gasp from the audience, followed by stunned silence.

I was about to run off in tears. This was the single most humiliating moment of my life.

And that's when the Greatest Magicians In The World started laughing and applauding. They stood up. Cheered.

This crowd was so used to the fake-out, that faking the fake-out was even more of a fake-out to them! They knew the coin was still in my right, so when I showed them it was actually in my left, they were shocked. Delighted.

I accepted their applause. I think I earned it.

Midway through my third curtsy, the security alarm went off. Shouts came from backstage.

Leave it to Baxter to ruin my moment of glory.

CHAPTER TWENTY-SIX
ALL WILL BE REVEALED!

Everyone hurried backstage and down the stairs.

The safe door was open, and inside it, we could see Baxter being held by a man with a big mustache. Detective Mustache!

"Look who I found inside the safe," Mustache said. "Snuck right in. Guess thievery runs in the family."

"The safe was open," Baxter said. "Obviously an attempt to lure me inside and incriminate me!"

"Oh, you're incriminated, all right," Mustache said. "You're about to be incriminated all the way to JAIL!"

"What for?" I asked. "He hasn't done anything illegal!"

Mustache laughed. "He's under arrest for the theft of the Crystal Ball of Nostradamus! Clearly, he's mastered the ability to open the safe undetected."

The magicians behind me muttered and murmured.

"You know he didn't take the Crystal Ball," I told him, straight to his mustache. "He was states away from here. You were following us then."

"He's a magician," the Detective said. "I'm pretty sure he can teleport across the country. I've seen that sort of thing before. It's called a Port-a-Porter."

I rolled my eyes. Sucker.

"And now," the Mustache continued, "this boy is going into police custody..."

The Mustache scanned the crowd of magicians. "Unless someone here wants to make a confession to keep him out of jail?"

The Grand Gurus of Gujarat stepped forward from the pack of befuddled and shocked magicians. "You can stop now," one of them said.

And then the Gurus pulled off their beards and turbans, and the faces under the turbans were two I recognized.

So did Baxter. "Mom! Dad!"

I had to look away because I was allergic to something that was making my eyes water up.

But the Mustache Detective wasn't so sentimental. "The criminal always returns to the scene of the crime!"

"Wait a minute," I said. "You really did open the safe so that you could trap Baxter and draw them out, didn't you?"

"What if I did?" he sneered.

"That's entrapment!" I said, remembering a word I'd heard on a police show before. And that made me stop and think for a second. A police show... what was it about a police show...?

Mustache went on. "Now is a good time to tell us how you run through walls," he said. "Assuming it really is a trick and not actual witchcraft!" And he pulled out his pad and pen and flipped it like a baton.

And then it all fell together. I'd seen that little pen-twirl before. On television, and again recently. Twice recently.

"Waitaminute," I said. "You're not a real police detective!"

Mustache looked suddenly concerned. "I am too," he said, and pulled out his badge again. "See?"

I looked at the badge, saw the number on it.

Badge number — 5150!

"That's not your badge," I said. "That badge belongs to Bobby Popcorn, NYPD!"

He backed into the safe again, his mustache bristling. "I don't know what you're talking about," he said.

Baxter stepped forward. "Oh, yes you do," he said, and reached up and ripped the mustache right off the so-called Detective's face. "Jackson Plateau!"

"I knew it was you," Baxter said, "as soon as you revealed you had respect for a charlatan like Vinny Vision."

"Hey!" came Vinny Vision's voice, from the back of the crowd. He sounded a little offended. "Words hurt."

"No true magician could believe in that poppycock," Baxter said, and darned if he didn't sound like the Baxter of old again. "Just as no police detective is foolish enough to believe people can really walk through walls!"

"Okay, okay," Jackson Plateau admitted, "so I faked being a policeman... is that a crime?"

"As a matter of fact," I put in, "I think it is."

"That doesn't change," Jackson Plateau went on, "that the Crystal Ball of Nostradamus was taken from a locked safe, and the Bunkhouses were the only ones who could've taken it!" He pointed a finger at Baxter's parents. "I'm making a citizen's arrest!"

"What evidence do you have?" Baxter asked.

Jackson Plateau counted off on his fingers. "A locked safe, the Bunkhouses disappear in the middle of a show, while they're in the water tank," — he looked at Baxter — "another trick that must run in the family."

Uncle Manny patted Baxter on the shoulder. "That was a really flawless vanish, son." Baxter looked proud.

"And then," Jackson Plateau continued, "the Crystal Ball was removed from the locked safe, and nothing was left behind but a puddle of water." He looked at Uncle Manny and Aunt Winnie. "Obviously dripped by the people who had just escaped out of a water tank!"

"Seems pretty solid," I heard Vinny Vision say from the back of the room. I looked around and saw that he had somehow snuck a video camera in here and was taping the whole thing for his show.

I liked seeing that. I was going to look great on TV in the next couple of minutes.

"I wonder," I said, stepping forward and addressing the gathered magicians, and so that Vinny Vision could focus his camera on me. "I wonder if the Crystal Ball of Nostradamus was even in the safe."

"It was," Aunt Winnie confessed. "He showed us before the performance. He shows everyone the inside of the safe before a performance."

"Sure," I said. "He showed you a clear ball in the safe. But just because it was crystal-clear, that doesn't mean it was crystal." I turned to Jackson Plateau, but only about halfway, so Vinny Vision could get my profile. "Does it, Mr. Plateau?"

"I'm sure I don't know what you mean," Jackson Plateau said, looking around nervously.

"Don't you?" I asked. "Why don't you tell everyone here about your peculiar hobby? You know... ice sculpture?"

There was a satisfying gasp from the crowd. I could learn to enjoy this.

"That's right," I said. "Jackson Plateau is an expert ice carver. And a ball of carved ice would not only look like a crystal ball, but it would naturally melt in the safe during the show, leaving only a puddle of water and giving the perfect opportunity for Jackson Plateau to —"

I turned around to accuse him of framing the Amazing Bunkhouses in order to learn the secret of their greatest trick, but I stopped.

Because Jackson Plateau was holding a big sword he'd pulled off the wall of the safe.

Oh, boy. This was going to be bad.

CHAPTER TWENTY-SEVEN
CUT TO THE CHASE!

"The Scimitar of Salmanesh!" someone cried out. The voice was muffled, so it was probably Professor Somnambula in his gas mask.

"No one better stand in my way," Jackson Plateau said, pushing forward.

We all parted in front of him, stepping back. A guy with a sword tends to get that sort of treatment when he walks through crowds.

He backpedaled up the stairs, swinging the sword at us menacingly. "I'm going to get out of this place and no one is going to stop me."

He raced up the stairs and slammed the door on us. We heard it lock behind him.

Of the people trapped in the room, only Vinny Vision and I didn't pick handcuff locks at least seven times before breakfast every morning. That door was open almost as fast as if it hadn't been there at all.

Jackson Plateau was in the lobby when we caught up with him.

"Hey," he said when he saw us, clearly annoyed. "I thought I told you to stay there?"

"It's time you put the sword down," Baxter said sternly. "You're going to have to pay for what you did."

"Or at least apologize," I put in, and Baxter shot me a look that suggested he didn't appreciate my help.

"You'll never catch me alive!" Jackson Plateau said, and he charged out the front door.

We again ran after him, and saw him open the gate in the Hedges of Wonder, then look back at us and laugh.

"You haven't seen the last of Jackson Plateau!" he shouted, and ran through the gate.

And then we heard a loud thump, clank, and clatter.

Once we got through the gate, we found Jackson Plateau crumpled on the sidewalk on the other side of the Hedges, and the Bunkmobile parked at the curb, engine idling.

He was right, we hadn't seen the last of him.

There was a large, Jackson Plateau-sized dent in the side of the Bunkmobile where he had run into it, then rebounded like a bully's dodge ball off a wimpy kid, and fallen to the ground. He was groaning a little bit, but didn't look likely to be getting up anytime soon.

Uncle Danny stepped out of the Bunkmobile. "Hey," he said when he saw us. "You'll never believe it, Berni! I found a primo parking place at the curb, just like you said —"

And then he saw the dent in the side of his mobile home "hey, where'd that come from? Somebody'd better have good insurance!"

CHAPTER TWENTY-EIGHT
LAX AIRPORT

My parents decided to meet me at the airport so we could fly home together.

Baxter and Uncle Danny insisted on dropping me off. As he unloaded my bags, he took a call from Baxter's parents.

"Good news," Uncle Danny said. "They found the Crystal Ball hidden in an Ice Sculpture. But they've discovered that a bunch of other pieces in the safe are fakes. Apparently, he squandered all that Bobby Popcorn money on moisturizer and plastic surgery. Turns out, Jackie Pluto is a lot older than we thought."

"Jackson Pla—" I started, then stopped. What do I care what Uncle Danny calls that thief? "Too bad," I said. "I guess he'll always have reruns."

"Thanks for being my Lovely Assistant this summer," Baxter said, sticking his hand out for a formal handshake.

I slapped his hand aside with an eye-roll. "Lovely-schmovely," I said. "I'm your partner." And I gave him a big hug. He'd showered recently. It was cool.

"Oh, by the way," Baxter said. "Now that my parents are the new presidents of the Secret Order of Magic, we're going to go on a winter tour of Europe and visit the London Manor of Magical Mystery."

"London! That's where Dame Jocelyn Beauchamp lives!"

Baxter said, "Who?"

"She's the author of my favorite book series," I told him. "Tales of the Witches Boarding School!"

"Oh no," Uncle Danny said. "Not again."

I looked at Baxter. "Again?"

He shrugged. "Well, I was thinking... I'll need a Lovely Assis —" He stopped and looked me in the eyes. "I'll need a partner."

I smiled. "Yeah. You bet you will. I've got a few new ideas about the act. What do you think about square dancing?"

"Um." He looked worried.

"Kidding! Kidding!" I put an arm on his shoulder. "See you soon, partner."

Baxter nodded, and it seemed like he really was happy about the prospect.

I grabbed my bag and headed inside. I could see my parents waiting by the ticket booth with tans and Hawaiian shirts and huge smiles.

I turned back to steal a last look at the Bunkmobile and my summer companions, but Uncle Danny and Baxter were gone.

Disappeared? Maybe, maybe not. I chose not to debunk this one. This summer was magical and no one could ever convince me otherwise.

I went to my parents, and we hugged, and I forgot I needed to forgive them for going to Hawaii without me.

But before we went anywhere, I dropped my bag and pulled my trusty fifty-cent piece out of my pocket.

"Hey, Mom and Dad," I said...

"Want to see a magic trick?"

See ya this Christmas!!

About the Authors

Jamie Nash is a writing fool. *Emphasis on **fool**.* He writes for grownups and for TV and movies and books and comics. He's busy typing up new stories at his home in Ellicott City, MD. Still want more? Check out his website www.jamienash.net or follow him on twitter @Jamie_Nash.

Pete Barnstrom writes and makes movies in San Antonio, TX. He likes cartoons and superheroes and science, and also some boring stuff, too. He'd be an astronaut if he didn't get motion sickness. If you like the same sort of stuff he likes, you can follow him on Twitter at @MistahPete

Made in the USA
Columbia, SC
14 December 2017